Central Line to Eziat

KENNETH PAYNE

Central Line to Eziat
Copyright © Kenneth Payne 2007
All rights reserved.

ISBN 978-184426-461-2

First published 2007 by
UPFRONT PUBLISHING LTD
Peterborough, England.

Printed by Printondemand-Worldwide Ltd.

Contents

Acknowledgements

The "Elegy to Ireland" in Chapter 4 was written by Francis Kendall-Husband a wanderer through Europe in the 1950s and 1960s. It was given by him to the author of this book in 1968, but may have been published elsewhere. In the context of this book, both his name and the events surrounding him have been changed.

Apart from this one exception, none of the characters in this book refers to any person, living or dead. Likewise the situations described have no connection with actual events.

I am deeply indebted to the inspiration provided by many friends; the Teams of Our Lady (the movement to help the spiritual growth of married couples); the Missionaries of the Poor (with whom I have worked for several short periods); and the community of Taize in France. Also, for the quotations in Chapter 8 by Teilhard de Chardin and Henri Boulad from his book "All is Grace" obtainable from Hidda Westenberger, A-9020 Klagenfurt, Gottesbichl 17, Austria. I should also like to thank Keith Wibley for his help with the cover design and Simon Potter of Upfront Publishing for his kindly help.

Finally, my thanks go to Katherine Coburn who had the onerous task of deciphering my scribble and to Lorna Foort for reading the proofs and making so many valuable suggestions.

Foreword

The Central Line tube cutting across the centre of London, was the first at its opening in 1900 and was known as the "tuppenny tube". After subsequent increases in the price of a ticket and several extensions in both directions, it became the Underground's longest line.

In its early days my father recalls being taken by his father, an inspector on the tube, to the cab in the front of the train and standing beside the driver. He was able to watch a pinpoint of light in the far distant tunnel gradually growing into a large orb and followed by the light of the next station. My father recounts that it was for him, at that time, an exciting moment and gave him a sense of being quite important.

In this book the Central Line becomes a symbolic basis for what could superficially be called the travel journal of a number of very different people. However, it is much more than a travelogue – as I have tried to show that we are all on a journey that involves every dimension of our being, physical, intellectual, emotional, spiritual and social. It is different for each one of us as is shown by the varied characters who move from despair and meaninglessness towards faith, hope, love and commitment. This finds its outcome beyond the end of the line at the remarkable place called Eziat.

Chapter 1 – Central Line

It was a Monday morning rush hour on the twentieth of June. The Central Line tube train curving through the centre of London was full. Each coach had its load of straphangers; those who were seated were reading their morning newspapers, mostly the cheap, gory and sexy tabloids. Some of the less fortunate, who were standing, were endeavouring to focus on their newspaper or book whilst the rest gazed downwards or at the shoulder or neck of the person just a few inches away from them. Very few experienced eye contact with their nearest neighbours.

Suddenly between Notting Hill Gate and Queensway the train reduced speed, the brakes gave a rough squealing sound and the train came to a halt. Those standing toppled forwards like a pack of cards, although fortunately no one fell to the floor as they were all so tightly packed. There were gasps and exclamations of alarm followed by silence for a few seconds until a woman's voice exclaimed "Good God, what happened?"

No answer was forthcoming but most people began making mundane comments to those near to them. After a few moments an announcement came over the speaker system:

"We apologise for what may be a short delay. I have been informed that someone has fallen onto the line at Queensway, the next station. We will start moving again as soon as possible"

"That's always happening," remarked the smartly dressed middle-aged lady who had already exclaimed. She was standing pressed against those around her, one of whom nodded and grunted in response, "Yes, it's one of the reasons for the double doors at Westminster and several other stations." The speaker was well-dressed in a dark blue pin-striped suit but he looked tired and depressed.

"Hope it's not going to be a long delay or I'll be late," remarked one young man. He was standing with two cycle panniers wedged between his legs. Near him another young man was seated with a large rucksack by his side. An attractive blond haired girl standing within sight of the latter was staring at him, clearly attempting to attract his attention. However in this she failed as he seemed preoccupied with his thoughts. She remarked in a voice loud enough for him to hear, "Say, does this happen often here in London?" By her accent she was probably from Australia. However, the young man with the rucksack, whose eye she seemed to be wanting to catch, was looking elsewhere.

Closer to her an elderly couple looked at each other anxiously. The husband glanced at the girl and nodded, "Occasionally," he said, and responding to the earlier young man's comment, his wife added, "And we've a doctor's appointment too." Her husband was leaning on a stick and looked ill and worried. By this time most of the people in the coach had begun talking with the exception of a few who were still buried in their newspapers.

After some minutes a further announcement was heard, "We may have to reverse to Notting Hill Gate Station. It seems there is still trouble at Queensway - apologies for this delay."

The smartly dressed lady again authoritatively addressed the passengers standing near her. "I do wish they'd clean up these trains. Just look at those papers and wrappings left here." She was standing just in view of a ledge by the window where several tatty papers and take-away cartons had been deposited. At that moment she also noticed the young man with his bulging rucksack and various appendages seated quite near to her. "And," she added in an even louder voice, "young people nowadays never think of offering their seat to an older person."

The pin-striped man, also near her, by-passed this comment and said, "It's very sad when someone despairs so much that they throw themselves onto the line,"

"But it might have been murder: someone may have pushed him - or her." It was a tall black man who was squeezed close to, and holding the waist of a white woman who had both arms around his waist and was gazing adoringly into his eyes.

"Where are you from?" asked another young man who had previously spoken and who was also standing close to the couple.

"I'm from Kingston, Jamaica," replied the black man. "Lots of murders there every day," he added.

At that point the train began to move backwards. There were gasps of relief and the various scraps of conversation that had begun a few minutes earlier either petered out inconclusively, or in a few cases, where a certain affinity had been recognised, continued for a while.

Arriving once again at Notting Hill Gate station, all were asked to leave the train and take alternative routes to their destinations. The Central Line would be closed for an indefinite period of time.

There was a concerted movement towards the doors. The young man who was seated and who had been verbally attacked by the smart standing lady, said apologetically to the pin-striped man who was nearest to him, "It was really impossible to get up and offer my seat to that lady. I was quite embarrassed, but I couldn't move and there was nowhere else to put my rucksack and other things."

"I shouldn't worry", the man replied, and then he added, "it looks as though you're going to have a good holiday."

"Yes, Corsica. Cheers – and thanks." And with that they parted, going in different directions.

The evening newspapers carried the headline,

'Suicide on the Central Line,' and in smaller print;

'Man ran across platform at Queensway underground station, threw himself onto the track and was killed instantly. He has yet to be identified.'

None of them on the train could have imagined the strange and varied cycle of events destined to bring them together again in three years' time.

Chapter 2 – Clothilde

Clothilde Fairlop was 43, tall with her hair meticulously rolled in a circle around the circumference of her head and neatly set in undulating waves with the roll. Her earrings hung low almost touching the collar of her light red silken coat. Her face, which had clearly confronted the mirror for more than a few minutes and probably considerably longer, was not heavily made up but nevertheless designed to accentuate a superior and 'I am better than you' expression as she glanced at the group of travellers pressed around her.

It was the morning rush hour on the Central Line across London and she stood looking as if she really felt that the whole carriage should be hers. There was little space around her, although she seemed almost untouchable and as if it would be irreverent even to brush an arm against her sleeve.

Clothilde, behind her haughty appearance, was deep in thought. She had noticed a couple standing in close embrace a metre from her. The girl was white, the man black. Clothilde recalled the time when she had had her arms around Harry soon after they had first met on an island in Greece. They were not black and white, but they were very different in temperament and background. She wondered what had drawn this couple together and she wondered what had drawn her and Harry together.

Clothilde came from a professional family. Her father had been the headmaster of a two thousand strong secondary school and her mother a ballet dancer with Sadlers Wells. Clothilde was the only child, born after they had been married some twelve years. She had sometimes wondered if her late conception had something to do with constrictions in her mother's anatomy through some of those contorted movements demanded by the ballet.

Harry Fairlop by contrast, was the youngest of eleven. He came from a working class Glasgow family. His father had been in ship-building – an ordinary job that hardly allowed him to pay the rent and feed his wife and hungry family. He had died just before drawing the state pension when Harry was on the point of leaving school. Harry applied for work at the ship-builder's yard and for ten years he took over his father's work. However, it wasn't to his taste and perhaps it was the smell of the sea that clung to the big ships and the tales he heard from the seamen in The Star and Anchor that inspired him to apply for the job of courier advertised in a travel agency. It was one of his young drinking pals who had heard of it whilst on a cheap package holiday to Rhodes. Harry had applied, and to his surprise, been accepted without an interview. By then he was 35 years old.

In fact 'courier' was a misnomer. He had joined a small privately owned Greek boat, which plied between Rhodes and Symi. He had to use his English, or more accurately, his Scottish, to say a few words to enquiring tourists visiting Symi. This attractive island was an hour and a half North-West of Rhodes, but for the rest of the time he was told to perform a multitude of general maintenance jobs, look after the small bar which sold bottled beer, soft drinks and stale and sticky kataifi, and leap from boat to jetty to tie up and help passengers off.

It was on one windy day towards the end of summer that Clothilde, on holiday with some friends, had come to the bar wanting a coke. They had chatted for a while as she stood there sheltered from the strong wind, probably the Eastern flank of the Meltimi, which had suddenly sprung up. There had been an immediate vibrant attraction on both sides, and they had arranged to meet in Rhodes two days later. The limits of Clothilde's holiday plans and restrictions due to Harry's work, enabled them to have only three more encounters that summer. However, promises were made and Harry handed in his notice to the shipping company. It was nearly the end of the season, and his experiences enabled him to get a job as a waiter in a small Greek restaurant in London, just south of the river. The owner was a cousin of the captain of the Rhodes boat. Harry and Clothilde were passionately in love and arranged for a quick and immediate Registry Office wedding, settling down to married life in a tiny third floor flat over the 'Restaurant Yannis". To describe them as settling down would be an exaggeration and distortion of the reality. Their lives were turbulent from the start.

Harry worked irregular hours in the restaurant, waiting, washing-up, clearing the tables and floor and often preparing vegetables – anything, in fact, that Yannis, the owner demanded of him. Clothilde worked in a fashion shop in Bond Street. She not only served some of the well-to-do customers who patronised the shop, but quite often she herself had to don some of the newly-designed dresses in order to show them off. She was in her element doing this as she had undoubtedly inherited some of her mother's histrionic ability.

Their ways of life were very different.

It was as Clothilde was on her way one morning to the Bond Street shop that the train she was on had come to a sudden halt. She had a long day in front of her and later that evening after closing time, the proprietress had asked her to stay behind to try on some new dresses that had just arrived from Paris. She was not pleased to have to continue standing in the stationary and crowded rush-hour train.

In fact she was already thinking of herself dressed in the new fashions and perhaps Madame Boucher would even let her go home wearing one of them, just for that evening. She imagined herself sweeping in through the main door of Yannis' restaurant later in the evening and calling out, so that all eyes would be turned to her, "Darling I'm back," and she would then go to the staff door into the kitchen, "Darling, haven't you finished yet? I'm simply dying for something to eat and drink. Just pour me a gin and tonic: the customers won't mind waiting another couple of minutes." All eyes of those dining there would be focussed on her. Some of the regulars would know her, whilst others would wonder if it was the introduction to a late evening's interlude in an Anglo-Greek style.

However, she invariably disappeared as soon as Harry had obediently, although often sullenly, placed the gin and tonic in her hand. In the kitchen, he himself would then pour himself a further pint of beer. He had usually consumed three or more before Clothilde's return.

That evening, it was Monday the twentieth of June. Clothilde, though tired, had returned in high spirits and immediately went up to Harry, who was about to serve some customers and to his amazement instead of demanding a drink or commenting on the smell of beer on his breath, said in almost a pleading tone of voice "Harry, let's get away from here for a break. I'm in need of it. It's going to be fairly slack in the shop for a few weeks, and it'll do us both good." She added the last phrase as an after thought. Harry, for a moment looked quite taken aback and surprised.

After a moment he said, "OK, but I'll have to speak with Yannis." Then he added, "but where shall we go?"

"I've never been to Germany," said Clothilde. "What about the Rhine?"

"Yes", thought Harry, "perhaps that would be a good thing to do." They had seemed to be drifting apart over the past months, so a week together could help to sort out their relationship – perhaps. He wasn't quite sure, but it would be worth a try. Besides the German beer was good and there'd be no shortage of it in the Rhineland.

"I'll see what I can find on the internet," replied Harry aloud.

Thus it was that their respective absences from work, Clothilde from the Bond Street fashion shop and Harry from his employment with Yannis, were negotiated; a small hotel in Konigswinter was booked for bed and breakfast for a weekend just two weeks hence, and their tickets arranged.

The time soon arrived and they left by air on the Saturday morning and arrived at their hotel which was situated within view of the Rhine with the hills in the background. At first all seemed to go well and the following morning, Sunday, they were late down for their typically German breakfast of a variety of cold meets, cheese, yoghurt, black bread, sausages, stewed fruits and an assortment of jams, honey and raw fruits, all to be washed down with coffee or tea.

It was then that Clothilde began to wonder how they would occupy themselves for the whole weekend. Why had she suggested this? Certainly a trip on the Rhine would be worth while, but what else was there? She sensed already that it was a place for indulging in drink and this would hardly be good for Harry, nor indeed for herself. They agreed to have a walk around the town. It wasn't yet the moment to talk seriously about themselves, so their conversation comprised mundane remarks about the contents of the shops and the prices advertised for lunches and suppers in the innumerable restaurants.

They came to an outdoor bar, sat down and Harry ordered a beer. Clothilde decided to have a cold fruit juice from the bar where they were seated. They could see a view of the Drachenfels, the nearby hills overlooking the Rhine. The foothills were swarming with people and in Konigswinter itself there seemed to be ever-increasing crowds of people moving up and down the streets. Young couples embraced as they walked along, the girls scantily clad in shorts with shoulders and mid-riffs bare, inviting a touch or caress from their male partner; some had removed their shirts; many were clearly the worse for drink. The Rhine wine was potent, especially when imbibed by the English who were unaccustomed to it. There was a saying, 'the wine and the heat go to your head and your feet'. However it was not only the foreign visitors who were somewhat the worse for wear. One young Fraulein was being hauled along by four beefy German youths who were finding it difficult to steer a straight path down the middle of the pedestrianised street. The girl was not being treated at all gently, but because of her own alcoholic state, was probably unaware of exactly what was happening.

Suddenly Harry stood up and announced abruptly to Clothilde that he was going to find a newsagents where he could buy an English paper and before Clothilde had an opportunity to reply, he was striding purposefully down the street. She continued to sip at her cold iced fruit juice lost in thought, wondering about Harry. Raucous loud voices mingled with the notes of an accordion from an adjacent bar. Everyone seemed to be talking twice as loudly as normal and above all, nearby church bells began to peel out reminding all and sundry that it was Sunday, the day when one should be turning to God.

By way of contrast to this Clothilde was thinking that these were times when she hated Harry... oh she was so mixed up in her feelings – she even wanted to kill him. Why had she married him? They really weren't suited.

What was he doing now? Doubtless he had found another bar and was imbibing in more glasses of liquor. If she waited for him much longer she could foresee exactly the state in which he would eventually return – that is if he even remembered where he had left her.

The church bells continued peeling loudly and this reminded Clothilde that Harry had been brought up a Roman Catholic and once, just before they were married, he had muttered something about the Catholic church not recognising the marriage of a Catholic in the registry office, but he had added that he wasn't really bothered about that.

On another occasion, after they had had a really big row, Harry had accused her of having sex with dozens of men before he met her and that it even continued to happen in the Bond Street shop. They had both lost their tempers and she had brutally and sarcastically told him that he should go to confession or seek professional advice for his drink problem, to which suggestion he became even more angry. And then, quite suddenly he had subsided and remarked that he had only ever found one priest whom he could ever talk to, a certain Father Christopher who was in a community somewhere in North London, but he had no intention of going to see him. He didn't need to.

Yes, thought Clothilde, he really did need help – and, she decided, so did she: need to speak with someone about all her problems. Would she and Harry ever come close together again? Had they ever been really close? Had it just been a desperate sort of infatuation, coming a little late in life for each of them?

At this point she became aware of a group of Americans at the next table and within ear-shot. She could clearly hear the twang of their accent. Americans anywhere, she thought, would be within ear-shot.

"Say Laura, do you know where I was on September eleventh 01? Boy, I could easily not be here right now." The speaker, a big bellied, round-faced man of about 50 did not wait for a reply but continued, "I was in a cab that only two minutes previously had passed right by those twin towers." He was addressing his remarks to two ladies seated at the same table and facing him. The one whom Clothilde guessed was Laura was heavily made-up, had long dangling ear-rings which just touched against her half exposed shoulders below which a bright loose fitting yellow dress fell almost to her ankles. The other lady was more quietly and discreetly dressed and by the expression on her face clearly wished their conversation had not taken the turn it had.

14

"Darling," she almost shouted, "I know it was a frightening experience, but I do wish you wouldn't keep reminding me of it so often. After all, we're here on holiday" and she gave an even louder emphasis to the "hol" of the last word.

"Laura", she said turning to her companion, "I just wanna go to the rest room, and then we might look at that fancy goods store we passed earlier. Honey," she turned to the man who by then Clothilde guessed might be her husband, "we'll both be back in a while: see you here."

As they left Clothilde looked once again at the crowds passing wondering if Harry would appear. However, her attention was almost immediately diverted back to the neighbouring table as its remaining occupant had turned towards her,

"Hi ma'am," he said, "I see you're alone, and that's just my situation for a while. D'ya mind if we talk?... You seem just a bit, what shall I say, in need of company... perhaps looking for company?" He pulled his chair closer to her table. Clothilde cringed but her reaction went unnoticed. Apart from an innate dislike of loud-mouthed Americans she feared that if Harry returned with liquor in him and saw her talking with another man he would throw a fit.

"I'm just awaiting my husband's return," she said coldly. "He'll be here any moment." She both hoped this would be true and yet, in a way, she hoped it wouldn't be true. She did object to loud Americans, but on the other hand, she thought, for a change, she wouldn't mind talking to someone, anyone, other than Harry.

"My name's Guy," continued the American. "You know, I just love the way you English talk. I was sharing a taxi with an Englishman back in New York when that plane hit the tower on nine eleven. He was just saying to me, in a real Oxford accent, that…" Guy got no further. Harry suddenly appeared at the other side of the table. He flopped onto a chair red in the face and eyes bleary, banged his fist on the table and shouted

"So that's what yer bloody well do while I turn my back for two minutes! You bloody whore, you bitch!"

Clothilde was stunned with embarrassment and fright, although she had half anticipated that he would return and create a scene. Her acquaintance of the past few moments immediately rose from his seat and mumbled, "I'm sorry sir, excuse me- I was just passing the time of day whilst waiting for my wife. Pleased to have met you." He addressed the last sentence to Clothilde.

Harry grunted, slid his chair, with a dangerous movement nearer to Clothilde, spat on the ground in the direction of the retreating American who had clearly decided it would be best to move as far away as possible to the other side of the café, and continued his verbal battery. He started dragging up from the past incident after incident in which he claimed Clothilde had neglected him, ignored him, been selfish and greedy and driven him to drink.

Clothilde was familiar with the pattern of his attacks but usually it was within the four walls of their flat. Here in a popular tourists' café in the middle of Konigswinter with many English speaking people around them she was humiliated, ashamed and almost terrified.

Without saying a word, but with dignity and decision she rose from her chair and left him seated, his head slowly sinking to the level of the table. People had turned to witness the scene and she just caught sight of the waiter approaching the table, probably to make sure that Harry would settle up. She didn't wait to see what happened.

How was she going to survive a weekend of this she wondered? An hour later Harry staggered in to their room, flopped on to the bed and was immediately asleep.

Clothilde spent the afternoon meandering by the river watching the pleasure craft and envying some of the happy revelling holiday people. That evening she was back at their hotel and Harry had recovered. He was, as was usually the case, very quiet and clearly filled with remorse. She, in turn, said nothing and for the rest of the weekend neither communicated with the other beyond a few superficial pleasantries. That was until on their way in a taxi to the airport for the return journey on the Monday morning Clothilde said quietly, "We can't go on like this. What do you want to do?"

"I've been good since yesterday haven't I?" replied Harry

"Yes, but your drinking habits and abuse make big wounds in our relationship and I'm not prepared to endure much more of it."

They arrived at the airport at that moment, checked in, and were for the rest of the journey surrounded by people. Once back in their flat, both tired, no further conversation ensued and the following day they were back at work. The few days in Germany had not been the success for which she had hoped.

During the ensuing weeks Clothilde began to dislike returning at night to the run-down area of London South of the river. She became increasingly irritable and contumacious as she entered the restaurant. Harry would hardly ever have finished with customers and his various chores took another two or sometimes three hours, during which time he would invariably consume several pints of beer and anything else left over by customers.

Clothilde would retire to bed to sleep, except on one evening she had stayed on for a late night party with the staff of the shop. They were celebrating Madame Boucher, the manageress's birthday. Clothilde consumed quite a lot of alcohol and Madame Boucher had suggested she remained in her flat for the night.

She eventually returned to her own place early the following morning to find that Harry had been phoning the shop, the police and some of their friends and was wild with anger when Clothilde coolly entered with no apology, and even seeming quite pleased with herself. They had a vicious verbal battle which was not confined to words but bodies were thumped and household objects were thrown.

It was interrupted by the telephone persistently ringing. Harry stormed down to the restaurant and finally, after hesitating and trying to calm herself Clothilde lifted the receiver. It was her mother, Frances. She was sobbing. Clothilde could hardly make out what she was trying to say.

"Darling Clothilde," she finally sobbed out, "your father – he's dead – oh God!" Eventually Clothilde made out that her father had suddenly collapsed in front of the whole school whilst taking an Assembly.

Clothilde had one thought. She had to be with her mother. She threw some clothes in a suitcase, rushed downstairs, avoided Harry who was somewhere in the kitchen and took the tube to Hampstead Garden suburb, where her parents lived. Bereavement, being with her mother and helping with all the practical arrangements necessitated by the funeral, kept her fully occupied and she felt no desire to see or talk with Harry.

"He could go to the devil," she thought. He, in turn, made no attempt to try to contact her. She almost didn't mind.

The funeral had taken place. It had been a big affair with a large church overflowing with people, relatives, friends, staff and representatives from all the classes in the school. When it was all over Clothilde still felt that she had no inclination whatever to see Harry. Her mother's house was so much more comfortable than the cooped-up two rooms over Yannis' place. She was quickly getting used to life without Harry and enjoying it, although it was a sad time without her father and there was the task of trying to help her grieving mother.

Three weeks after the funeral, she decided to go back to collect her personal belongings. She still had the key and she crept in the back way when she thought Harry would be busy in the restaurant. In their flat, to her surprise, she found him sound asleep on the sofa with evidence of a quantity of drink having been consumed. She gathered her belongings and crept out again. He did not stir. She was relieved and felt no pity for him.

Living with her mother and sometimes working late at the shop however, soon palled. Frances, her mother, after they had been more than a few minutes together invariably began to cry. "Why had her darling husband died like that and so suddenly?" It would soon be winter. The evenings were becoming long and dark. She wished Clothilde were at home more often. Then one evening Frances was sitting looking out of the window, just thinking. There was a distant hum of traffic but she could see nothing except the tall, dark, evergreen hedge which successfully hid the road and the passers-by from the house. The high hedge had, years previously, been her idea. Now she wished it wasn't there. She wanted to see people, living people, and life. Why not go out then? Yes, that's what she would do. It was an unusually mild night. Yes, she'd go out for a walk on her own. Clothilde wouldn't be back for another two hours. She donned her thick black coat and small dainty hat which had a ring of small-netted baubles hanging some two inches below its rim.

As she began walking down the street towards the traffic junction she had no idea where she was going. There was a lull in the evening traffic. She decided to cross over and walk towards the nearby cemetery. That was where her darling was buried. She felt hot. Her black coat, which had been bought especially for the funeral with the thought of a cold church and an even colder cemetery, was too thick. She was conscious of being hot and as she stepped out into the road the net around the edge of her hat blew slightly and partly masked her vision to the right just as the number twenty-four bus swung round the corner from the cemetery road. Perhaps it cut the corner too quickly, or perhaps she hadn't quickened her pace sufficiently as she crossed to the opposite pavement. The driver braked but it was too late. She was struck down by the front near side wheel of the double-decker bus.

The next thing she was conscious of was lying in bed with white-clothed and masked doctors and nurses around her, vaguely conscious of tubes attached to various parts of her face and body until she drifted into unconsciousness again. The next time she surfaced, Clothilde was standing by the bed looking down at her. Then Frances seemed to be floating away from herself and softly calling out, "Goodbye Clothilde. I'm going to see my darling". She then seemed just to slip away as her breathing slowed and ceased altogether.

Clothilde was devastated. There was another funeral to arrange, on her own this time. She decided not to get in touch with Harry. She couldn't cope with any more emotional strain, so she arranged a quiet funeral with a small representation from her father's school, a distant cousin and a few friends.

In the weeks following the funeral Clothilde continued working at the shop, but her heart was no longer in it. The work began to seem tedious and even showing off a new style of dress seemed to pall. The different fashions ceased to thrill her.

She was settled in her parents' flat, but it was a lonely life. She had inherited all of her parents' property and savings which provided her with all she needed to live quite comfortably.

She decided to give up her work in the shop. She would have time to enjoy herself. But how and with whom? Both her parents had gone within a few months. She had put in for a divorce just after her father's death, but there was no one else who had appeared on the scene. She had a few friends and some distant cousins but no one whom she could describe as a close friend. She began to know the meaning of loneliness.

Then one day, Jeanette, a woman who lived in Paris and with whom she had, whilst at school, done an exchange, wrote to her inviting her to stay. They had only occasionally corresponded since leaving school, but Clothilde had enjoyed two good holidays in Paris and she had a vivid recollection of Jeanette's older brother, Pierre, whom at one time she thought might have been interested in her. She remembered him as being slightly taller than herself with large brown eyes, tidy close-cropped blond hair and a way of laughing heartily every time he made a mistake when attempting to speak English. She had not seen him for eight or nine years. He was undoubtedly married by now.

All these thoughts and memories passed quickly through Clothilde's mind, and coupled with a deep hollow of loneliness, she decided then and there to book her seat on the Eurostar and spend a week in Paris.

A week later Jeanette met her at the Gare du Nord. Unlike Clothilde, she had not got married, and was living in a flat in the Latin quarter quite near the river. Her brother Pierre, spent part of the time there and part at his work with the United Nations in Geneva.

Jeanette and Clothilde spent the first three days catching up on each other's news, visiting some of the fashionable shops, walking in the Tuilleries and in the narrow side streets of the left bank. Clothilde was happy. She loved the village-like atmosphere of those intimate parts of Paris away from the more formal boulevards. Paris was so different from London. People lived in flats over shops and behind the shops, flats centred on attractive little courtyards which were often so quiet that you could imagine yourself in the heart of the country. The fact that so many people lived in the centre of the city was the reason for less vandalism and the crime that is so often found in London, where the majority escape to the suburbs each evening leaving the centre an empty void.

One day they both decided to go out to see Monet's Garden at Giverny. One of Clothilde's favourite paintings was Monet's painting of the bridge; she had inherited a reproduction of it from her mother. It was raining a little when they arrived there but it cleared soon after their arrival leaving an almost uniform grey sky. The moisture on the flower petals seemed to accentuate the beauty and naturalness of the place. The garden was more English in style than French; Monet had wanted the vegetation to appear quite natural. Jeanette commented that perhaps they were seeing it better in the wet as the colours seemed to sparkle so.

Before leaving they followed the sign to Claude Monet's grave situated just behind the village church, however the names on his family grave were indecipherable covered as they were with dirt and the corrosion of the stone.

"His best memorial," remarked Clothilde, "must surely be his paintings".

On the fourth day Clothilde announced that she wanted to go to the Rodin museum. Jeanette was unable to accompany her, and anyway, she wasn't particularly interested, so Clothilde took the Metro, the line 13 towards St. Denis, finding that she had to get off at Varenne.

As she was standing surveying with her usual slightly contemptuous attitude the kaleidoscope of people standing around her, she noticed, towards the other end of the carriage a circle of people all standing a certain distance from a figure clinging to one of the upright posts. It was a man with his head drooping downwards, wearing an old overcoat which was torn at the collar, half way down the sleeves and at the pockets, from both of which protruded the tops of dark brown beer cans. His hair was long and matted and merged with his unshaven cheeks and chin. As she looked she was horrified to observe a movement all over his head and then she noticed a similar disturbance around the neck and shoulders of his coat. He was alive! There were lice everywhere; little wonder that the people standing near him had edged away.

The train stopped at St. Francis Xavier. People got off and others got on. She had one more station to go. With the new influx of people the man she had noticed had half turned and moved much nearer to her. He was now only a metre and a half away, clutching another of the carriage's uprights. A piece of card hung from his neck. On it was written "Je suis sans travail" (I am without work). Some of the letters were cramped together and the first two words seemed to read "Jesus sans travail" (Jesus without work). She could almost see his face. No, it couldn't be! At that moment he looked up from the floor at which he had been staring and caught her eye. It was Harry, and he had recognised her.

The train was slowing down. She had to get out. She would have got out anyway, even if it had not been her stop. The wave of horror that had shaken her to begin with was increased by a slight trace of pity. This was the man she had once embraced, had slept with, had loved – or had she, did she?

The train had stopped. Her hand fumbled in her bag and she found a Euro. She threw it over towards him, rushed to the doors of the train and almost ran to the exit stairs. Someone standing near the confused and crawling figure picked up the Euro and let it drop into Harry's pocket. It rattled metallically against the beer can. Harry gave a half smile and a tear ran down his cheek as he looked at the fast retreating figure of Clothilde who had gone to view the naked stone bodies of the Rodin sculptures.

When eventually Clothilde returned to London she was haunted by the remembrance and sight of Harry. She would wake up at night imagining she could hear the sound of her coin hitting against his beer can. She was often unable to sleep thinking continually of that day on the Paris metro and Harry....

She would look sometimes at the Monet picture of The Bridge and she remembered once her mother saying that Monet should have painted two people standing on the bridge as she and Clothilde's father had once done, two people coming from different directions with different outlooks but coming together, and being always together there on the bridge, looking at the beauty around them and seeing their reflection in the water below, seeing themselves as they truly were. But, Clothilde thought, she and Harry had never been like that – they had come from opposite directions but never been together on the bridge and never really seen into the depths of each other's minds. But even so...

One morning she awoke having had a vivid dream of herself talking with a man whom she thought was a priest. He was laying his hands over her head and seemed to be praying. As she awoke from her dream she remembered Harry having mentioned a priest with whom he had once thought of speaking. His name was Christopher. Clothilde wasn't a Catholic, hardly a Christian, she supposed, but that probably wouldn't matter. Perhaps she could find him and talk to him. How could she locate him? She decided on the off chance to call in at the Catholic Church she sometimes passed in her lunch break. It was quite near Bond Street.

That same day she rang the bell at the Church office at St. Patrick's in Soho and the secretary she spoke with checked in a directory and told her that the priest in question could be found at a place called Eziat. He lived just beyond the last station on the Central Line and, if Clothilde would phone him, she felt sure he would see her. He had the reputation of being of great help to people in trouble and with problems. Clothilde there and then decided to go to see him.

Chapter 3 – The Choice

The flight from Heathrow to Nice left Heathrow at midday. Damian Debden, with a bulging rucksack and various appendages attached including a small tent, sleeping bag and other items intended for two weeks in Corsica, had only just managed to catch the plane. He had been delayed on his way to the airport by an accident on the underground. Someone had fallen on the line at Queensway station and he had been diverted.

Damian's father was Irish, originally from Cork while his mother came from Dublin. Some would maintain that this was not a good combination. However their marriage had given rise to eight children of whom Damian was the youngest. His father, like many of his countrymen, indulged frequently in cracking jokes, often against himself. However this time it was not against himself as he bid his son farewell on this particular morning. Damian was anxious to be away when his father insisted on telling one of his stories.

"Don't be like the American tourist, my son," he said, "you know, the one who got lost in the country just outside Cork, and, to make matters worse, he had no watch. Then he saw a young lad milking a cow in the field, and he gave him the directions back to the hotel. He said to him, 'Would you have the correct time?' The boy said 'Sure,' and then he lifted the cows udders high, and said, 'it's three o'clock.' The American said 'That's amazing. How can you tell the time by lifting the cow's udders?' The boy said,

'Easy, when I lift the cow's udders high enough, I can see the village clock.' Ha, Ha," concluded Damian's father. "Tell that to your friends in Corsica."

Then he couldn't refrain from adding, "Be careful of those lunatic French drivers, because if you get run down crossing the road and get both your legs broken, I don't want you to come running to tell your mum and me…. Ha, Ha," he added.

With these words Damian finally set off for the airport. He arrived at Nice an hour before catching the boat for the last part of his journey to Corsica. "It would be good," he thought, "to see the famous, 'La Promenade des Anglais', before heading for the port." Just as he caught sight of the sea and what he thought might be the beginning of the promenade, two events occurred, one of which was destined very nearly to change the whole course of his life.

He was twenty-two years old, good-looking with straight blond hair which had become somewhat in disarray from his journey. His holiday to Corsica was by way of being a celebration after sitting his final degree exams in modern European history.

Why had Damian chosen Corsica for his holiday? He couldn't really explain his choice, except that he wanted to see at first hand the sort of place that had given birth to that great enemy of England, Napoleon. The Napoleonic war, Waterloo and nineteenth century European history had occupied much of his studies.

Napoleon, he guessed, as he approached the sea, must have known Nice. However, before pursuing further this line of thought, he espied a stand-up urinal, one of the old-fashioned types once common in France, prominently situated on the street corner. It comprised a central metal column, some five feet in diameter around which was set a gully thigh height from the ground. Surrounding this was a circular metal screen which allowed just enough space for a man to stand and satisfy his needs in the gully. His head and shoulders and the lower part of his legs only would be visible to passers-by. Damian entered the fairly confined space giving access to the centre of the urinal just as another young man was about to exit. At that moment Damian realized that he was able to move neither forward nor back. His laden and protruding rucksack had successfully jammed him in the opening. He struggled and then burst out laughing, whilst the man about to come out grinned and said in English, "Shall I give you a push?"

"Oh, thanks," replied Damian, "that might help"

The stranger caught hold of Damian's rucksack, half twisted it round and pushed. Damian moved backwards, and they both laughed.

"These confounded French urinals," said Damian. "Anyway, thanks a lot. I see you're English too"

"Yes," replied the other, "I'm Jim – well, James Woodford really, but everyone calls me Jim. And you?"

"Damian Debden – or sometimes known as Dee Dee for short."

"It's good to meet a fellow countryman. Where are you off to?" responded Jim.

"Look, if you don't mind, I'll have another go at getting in there," said Damian, "and if you'll wait a minute we can then talk."

"OK. I'll wait on this bench. Leave your rucksack with me this time," he added laughing.

Damian was beginning to think that his bulky rucksack was becoming an encumbrance. The lady on the underground had made a rude remark about him taking up too much room with his luggage and not standing up. And now it had caused him to be jammed in a French loo.

When Damian returned he sat down beside James, extracted a half-consumed bottle of coca-cola and offered it to James. "I'm off to Corsica as I want to do a little first-hand research on Napoleon, and I'm also just interested in seeing what the island's like"

"You're catching the night boat then?" said Jim, "I am, too. I'm actually spending most of the summer there in a Franciscan monastery up in the hills at Calacuccia"

"That sounds great," responded Damian.

"Yes, and the priest there would make you very welcome if you wanted to stay for a bit."

"Well," said Damian, "that would be good, in fact," he added, "I'm actually a Catholic and am thinking tentatively of becoming a priest."

"Well," rejoined Jim, "I'm probably going in the opposite direction. You see, I'm not really a Christian, but they put up with me in the monastery. I think I was baptised something or other as my mother thought it would be good to 'get me done', as she said, but I think I lean more towards the Buddhist idea of religion."

"Perhaps we'll chat more about that later if we're going to travel together," interrupted Damian, "I think we'd best be going towards the port and find the boat for Corsica".

As they walked along they viewed critically the 'Promenade des Anglais' but found it, as Jim said, a 'let down'. Arrived at the night ferry, they each headed for the semi-padded seats in the rather Spartan lounge. As they were sorting out their belongings and endeavouring to make themselves comfortable, a young girl of about twenty or so, also with a bulging rucksack came and sat alongside them.

"You look English," she remarked to Damian. "You don't mind if I curl up here, do you?" she then asked with a distinctly Australian accent and added, "I'm travelling on my own and it makes me feel more secure to have someone who's English nearby. By the way," she added, "I'm Shirley."

"And I'm Damian."

"And I'm Jim. We're also travelling simply. We only met up just a while ago."

"That's terrific," she replied and then went on to explain that she had been a student at the London School of Economics but more recently had just returned from Brisbane where she had been at her mother's funeral. This she related in quite a matter of fact way. "I couldn't stay on with my father," she added, "we don't really get on very well: he's such a gas bag!"

Then, after a pause and looking carefully at Damian, she said, "You know I've an idea I saw you in London yesterday. Weren't you on that train that was held up because someone had fallen on the line?"

"That's right," replied Damian, "you've got good eye sight," not wishing to admit that he had not noticed her. He had, in fact, been more concerned that he wouldn't miss his flight. They went on chatting together for a while until they noticed that several other passengers near them had spread themselves across the seats and some were already asleep.

"We'd better be quiet and follow suit," whispered Damian.

Soon after six o'clock the next morning the boat docked in at Bastia and the three of them decided to find somewhere for a coffee and something to eat. Damian caught himself continually looking admiringly at Shirley, who also seemed to be attracted to him.

After having satisfied their stomachs they wandered for a while around the streets of Bastia. However their first impression of it was of shells and filth: the beach was dirty and everywhere seemed to smell of an unpleasant blend of gaulois, garlic and rotting flesh – presumably that of animals! It was not a place in which to linger.

After discussion they all three agreed to take the narrow gauge train up into the hills, where Jim had been staying. The rail track twisted and turned its way through undergrowth and weeds. The driver seemed to be attempting to see how fast he could take the train whilst still keeping the wheels on the track. It was a three hour trip to Calve, a former Genoese citadel which, in mid summer was being enjoyed by a considerable number of German visitors.

It was whilst exploring some of the side streets of Calve that one of Damian's sandals fell to pieces. He had hoped they would last out his holiday. All three started hunting for a suitable repairer as Damian had no spare footwear. Finally they found a little old man in a tiny workshop squeezed in between two shops. He was hammering away at a shoe last, but on approaching him, he agreed to do the necessary repair immediately. It would take half an hour.

James decided to go off to browse in a nearby bookshop whilst Damian and Shirley agreed to sit down and quench their thirst in a café as Damian was hopping along with one foot bare.

By this time they both realised they were enjoying each other's company. Their conversation went with a swing. Damian was finding Shirley vivacious, very natural and open, and essentially a good person. She seemed to be good, not in any priggish or prudish sense, but when she looked directly at him it aroused in him the assurance that all was right with the world. He had a sense of security.

They shared something of their stories and Damian made the discovery that Shirley was also a Christian. This made him tell her that he had thought of one day becoming a priest. She had greeted this revelation with interest and had remarked, "Think well about it first. You would probably make a good one, but it's a very big step to take."

Damian responded to the advice by taking hold of Shirley's hand and squeezing it and leaving his hand joined to hers. He felt quite at home with her although they had met each other only the day before.

Already a certain tension, a conflict was developing in Damian's mind concerning his desire to become a priest. Was he becoming infatuated with Shirley?

These things happened: love at first sight.... It had happened to him before. They were certainly getting on very well together and he was unable to take his eyes off her. Her shimmering blond hair and her slightly bronzed skin appeared to shine in the sunlight, and matched his own; her eyes seemed to respond lovingly, he thought, to his own gaze. If only, he thought, the Church would become more open to the possibility of a married clergy. After all, there always had been married clergy in the Eastern rite church and they were recognised as part of the Roman Catholic Church under the Pope. Would the Pope change?

It was after all an unjust situation allowing the ordination of married men from Anglican clergymen who had been in the Catholic Church for less than a couple of years, and yet not ordaining those who had served all their lives as Catholics, perhaps brought up a family and gone through the ups and downs, the slings and arrows of outrageous fortune in the cause of the Church and of the Lord, and yet could not be ordained.

Then, he thought, it wasn't only the question of married priests but also that of women priests. He could appreciate that there might be cultural and psychological reasons against this but not theological ones. Perhaps if he went to the seminary he would learn differently.

Then he thought of all the poverty, homelessness and loneliness, and so much suffering in the world. It was surely more important to deal with that than to lose sleep on theological niceties, because that is what they seemed to him to be. He still had these thoughts racing through his mind and was sharing some of them with Shirley when she looked at her watch and suggested that it was perhaps time for them to collect his sandal.

They all three met up at the friendly shoe-repairer's shop and with Damian properly shod they decided to take the train on to Francardo. There, after an hour's patient wait at the roadside hoping for a lift, the only signs of life or activity were four vehicles and an old lady carrying her shopping home. The latter stopped for a brief chat, questioning the young people as to what they were doing. When they explained to her that they were hitch-hiking to the monastery she immediately admonished them, "Oh dear," she said, "be very careful: the drivers in Corsica are terrible – too fast and dangerous." They were just going to the monastery they told her. "Oh dear," she replied, "those priests will work you to the bone if you stay there."

"But after that we'll be going down to the sea at Ajaccio."

Her face changed again, "Be very careful," she repeated, "it can be very dangerous swimming off Corsica."

At that they quickly thanked her for her advice, as a 'mazeout' rounded a bend, stopped, and the driver invited them to get in. The old lady waved to them at the same time frowning and shaking her head.

The driver seemed to be glad to have people with whom to talk. He told them that he lived in Corte, which was beyond Calacuccia where they were hoping to stay. He then went on to tell them that he had been a van driver in Paris, but he loved Corsica and was glad to be back in his native town. He hated the mainland and loved every inch of Corsica. The real French, he claimed, were really Corsican, though very few recognised this, least of all the French government. In Corsica they more or less ruled themselves. Whilst elaborating on this theme they were driving through a spectacular gorge in the mountains and their friendly driver seemed to be from the same school as the train driver, with little coordination between speed and bends in the road. They experienced the truth of the remark: the English and Americans have long been convinced that a car travels less quickly than an aeroplane whereas the French and most of the Latins still seem determined to prove the contrary.

He seemed sorry to have to leave them when they eventually arrived at Calacuccia and stopped in front of the Franciscan monastery which was situated just off the road and overlooking a small lake. Before leaving him and after thanking him, he leaned out of the van window and said, "Remember there are two important sayings in France:

'La vie est dure:
Les femmes sont chêres
Les enfants facile a faire.'
("Life is hard: women are dear and children are easy to come by")
'Faute de mieux: on se couche avec sa propre femme.'"
("for want of better, one goes to bed with one's own wife.")

With this profound advice in mind they rang the bell at the monastery door. There they were welcomed by the two priests who lived there, James introducing Shirley and Damian. James explained to the others that he would probably have to be busy with various practical jobs in the house and garden, as he'd been away for a few days and that was the condition for letting him spend part of his vacation there. This meant that Shirley and Damian would be left to amuse themselves and perhaps explore the region.

The nearby lake was man-made and although the water level was low, it was possible to swim in spite of the fact that, being at an altitude of some 800m, it was cold. Damian and Shirley nevertheless enjoyed a short swim and continued discovering that they had a lot in common. Both were involved in amateur dramatics and were interested in history. Their obvious attraction to each other was increasing by the hour, and the following day one of the priests offered to drive them both to a forestry station from which they could walk – and he assured them that it was an easy 'promenade' to the lac de Nino. This turned out to be in parts a rough and steep path until after two and a half hours climb, they sat down under a clear sky with the lake before them, to eat their packed lunch.

They were admiring the splendid scenery and enjoying each other's company when Damian felt impelled to say, "You know, Shirley, you must realise that I've become very attracted to you. You know, I really like you enormously."

Shirley took his hand, squeezing it. "Yes I guessed that, and I feel like that about you, too."

"You know, I feel almost torn in two, and yet it's crazy because we've only known each other a few days," continued Damian. "The Catholic Church, as you know, won't accept a married clergy – at least not in this part of the church, although there are signs that this may change in the future; but that's no help to me."

"Although we're attracted to each other," Shirley said after a moment, "we don't really know each other very well yet, do we?"

"True, but that could be remedied," replied Damian.

"We could both meet up again, soon, back in London."

"That would be good," said Shirley, "and you will have to continue to think seriously about this question of the priesthood," she added.

The return route was even more difficult, and they took the wrong track down. By then it was towards the end of the afternoon. Mist was gathering and there was barely an hour of daylight left. After a while, and with Damian having a good sense of direction, they retraced their steps to near the lake and found the correct path, but before they reached the forest station and managed to beg a lift back to Calacuccia, it had become quite dark. This slight emergency and common fear brought them even closer together.

The following day Shirley and Damian decided to leave the monastery and hitch-hike on to Ajaccio. They bid grateful farewells to the two priests and to James, promising to keep in touch. At Ajaccio Shirley was to meet up and stay with friends, a French family who were staying there. Damian would pursue his interest in Napoleon and continue exploring parts of Corsica associated with the emperor. For both of them it was a sad moment when they came to part and go their separate ways, although they had promised to keep in close touch.

Mobile phones had become very much the order of the day and this made communication easier whilst they were both still in Corsica, so that less than a week later before either returned to England they managed to meet up again in Ajaccio.

Damian had with him his small tent and just outside Ajaccio they found near the sea an area of private land where an Italian couple were renting a small house. The couple agreed to Damian and Shirley camping there for one night. It was a pleasantly quiet field alongside the house. However, when Damian asked if they could have the use of a toilet, the reply of the Italian husband was a gesture which embraced the whole of the surrounding countryside.

In this way they had three wonderful days together before Shirley, and then a day later, Damian had to take their previously booked flights back to England.

They exchanged a sad and emotional farewell with promises to keep in close touch. Shirley had arranged to be with a family she knew in Liverpool and where she would begin work in the library. Damian was returning to his parents in Ealing and to a possible decision with regard to his future.

Two days after his return Damian received an e-mail from Shirley. It began 'Dearest of all,' and went on to say that she was counting the minutes until she would see him again. There were many other signs and expressions of her affection which Damian was quick to respond to in his reply. Phone calls, e-mails and text messages followed. E-mails in particular were a life-line for both of them. Every few weeks they arranged to meet at a small bed and breakfast place which was cheap and about half-way between London and Liverpool.

The intensity of their initial attraction had begun to wear off and had been replaced by a deeper and more profound relationship, and the question of the possibility of their lives being spent together was a frequent topic of conversation. Well over a year passed in this way, but Damian was continually haunted by thoughts of the priesthood which would involve being celibate.

Then one day when they were together Shirley announced, just as they were parting, that it would soon be the 20th of June, just two years since they had first been together on the underground train that was held up in London and when they had met on the boat to Corsica.

"Do you think we're going to be together for always?" she had turned to him and asked. "I need to know," she added, "I don't feel we can go on like this."

Damian had paused, hesitated, and replied, "I really don't know, I don't know."

She had turned, jumped into her car and was gone.

He suddenly began to feel almost trapped. Could he, would he ever get married? Yes, he did love Shirley. Their being together had been for short periods of time but they felt they now knew each other well. However, did they really know all about the other – enough to be able to live together always? He remembered his grandfather remarking to him on the occasion of his grandparents' golden wedding celebration, "You know, I'm still finding out things about your grandmother." And she could undoubtedly have made a similar comment.

"No", Damian found himself saying to himself, "I still don't know, and I really, deep down, am wanting to be a priest, to be able to follow Christ with my whole being and to spread the Good News that I believe in". The next day, after much thought and prayer and hesitation Damian decided to write. He sat down at the computer:

'My dearest Shirley, It is not easy to write this letter, and I know it is not going to be easy for you to read it. Yet, after having given it very grave thought, I feel it must be written…. You will have guessed by this what is coming. I have become increasingly convinced of the necessity of becoming a priest. This, I feel sure, is what God wants of me. It will mean giving up a lot to do this. It means, first of all, that our relationship can no longer be as it has been up to now. I know you will feel awful about this, as I do myself, and I am sorry that I am giving you all this pain and suffering. I should not have encouraged you as I certainly did. I am sorry for this. However, I am sure you will get over it, and hopefully, we will both be able to say that we've enjoyed together some fantastically happy times. However, don't just live on memories! I am sure you will meet someone who is much better for you than I was – someone who is more attentive and thoughtful and not so selfish. You know that you will always be very dear to me, and I send you, as always, my love and assure you of my prayers."

Shirley's reply came by return post: 'My dear Damian, So it is to be "ave atque vale", after all. I have complete confidence in the all-ruling power of God, and know that this is the way it was meant to be. Still between the Ave and the Vale, short though it was, I have been magnificently happy, and learned the greatest lessons of my life, and never for a minute will I ever regret our time together. I hope you won't either." She then concluded, "You will always know, that wherever you are, and whatever you are doing you will have my prayers (for the little they're worth) my friendship and my love. Shirley.

Damian was greatly moved when he read this. It was so understanding and remarkably generous. He then suddenly felt alone – alone but far from lonely. Yes, he thought, alone to pursue the tasks and way of life that he felt so sure was God's will for him.

Shortly after receiving Shirley's letter he decided it would be good to go to confession, to make a really fresh start. He went to the little Catholic Church at Theydon Bois where he'd previously spoken with an understanding priest, a Father Christopher, who had also counselled him. Father Christopher, or Chris as he preferred to be called, was available when Damian called. He was a man in his fifties with greying hair, a matching beard and a perpetual twinkle in his eye. He was fond of reminiscing and at one point in their conversation he began to recount to Damian how he himself had found life in the seminary some twenty years previously.

It was very different from nowadays, he recounted, and quite tough in many ways. The bishop had sent him to Saint Sulpice in Paris. He had never before been to France and he had to struggle with philosophy and other subjects, equally bewildering and profound, through the intermediary of a language with which he was only partly familiar. Meals comprised a very basic French menu: soup, a small thick hunk of undercooked meat with celery, potatoes or possibly a leaf artichoke and concluded with a cream concoction which he later found out was 'petit suisse'.

To accompany this there was an ample supply of bread which was not only eaten, but prior to that used for wiping your plate between courses. Often you would want a further piece of bread broken from the baguette and for this, because meals were eaten in silence, you would raise your knife in the air to attract the attention of whoever had the supply of bread in front of him.

At the conclusion of the meal your knife, fork and spoon had to be swilled in a bowl of warm water placed on each table and wiped on your serviette. By the time that most students were up to this stage in the meal, the one who was lector, the reader for the day, would, at a sign from the superior, bang on the table, conclude his reading and all would rise for the grace.

The first morning at breakfast talking was allowed. One of the French students asked Christopher in French if he'd slept well. Chris, not as proficient in French as he would have like to be replied, "Pas tres bien: cette nuit je vais changer ma maitresse!"

Chris's French was rapidly to improve, becoming fluent after a few months. He had also become accustomed to the frugal regime of food and the cheap wine which was available at the midday meal, replaced by beer for supper.

Father Chris might easily have continued reminiscing on his life in the seminary years ago, but then he pulled himself up and seemed to recall why he was recounting it all to Damian.

"I had been in love with a girl not long before I started at seminary," he said, "but once launched into life at Saint Sulpice, I knew I had made the right decision and I've been so completely happy and fulfilled in my life as a priest and," he added after a pause, "most of all latterly in my life as a member of the Eziat community. You see," he continued, "the bishop allowed me a few years ago to help a small group of people, a religious community working with the very poor in the Philippines, and then, when I returned to England I signed up as a full member of the community of brothers at Eziat."

Father Christopher stopped. He was obviously struck by a great idea. "Now that's what you could do," he said, "spend a few months, before making a final decision, working in a third world situation. It would be a great experience. You'd see the Church functioning in a situation of poverty, very different from the middle class bourgeois atmosphere of England or western Europe."

Damian was clearly interested but he was becoming mentally a little exhausted listening to all of this and by Father Chris's inimitable enthusiasm about life in a foreign seminary. He also really wanted to ask Father Chris about his present community that he had mentioned at Eziat.

"I'll have to think about it," he said.

"And pray about it," added Father Chris.

Three days later he received a letter from Father Chris. It said that he, Chris, had been thinking and praying about what they had discussed and he felt that six months or so in the Philippines with the 'Brothers of Jesus' would be for Damian, an excellent preparation for whatever it was that God wanted of him. In Naga City in the Philippines, he said, Lepers, AIDS sufferers and many abandoned children amongst others, were all being helped. Chris ended his letter by adding once again, "Pray about it!" Damian was stunned when he read this and it occurred to him that Father Chris hadn't really got his two feet on the ground because he said nothing about the air fare necessary to travel to any of the places where the brothers worked. If God willed it, then it would happen, Father Chris had said, and "pray about it," which Damian had done but without very much conviction.

Two days later he developed a nasty patch of eczema on his foot and he decided that he would have to see the doctor. It was something he was occasionally prone to. Anyway this seemed to put a lid on any idea of going to the Philippines.

His appointment was for 9:30am the following morning. He arrived at the surgery in Acton in good time and seated himself in the waiting room next to an elderly lady on her own. She turned to him and remarked, "This is a gloomy room, isn't it? However, I've always found Doctor Farthing very kind and knowledgeable and helpful."

"Yes," responded Damian cheerfully, "I think he's a good doctor, although I've only seen him once before and I've only a small problem: just a slight outbreak of eczema."

"Oh, he'll sort that out for you," rejoined the lady. As she turned away, Damian noticed that she had long dangling ear-rings, her neck was wrinkled suggesting that she was well past middle age, and he thought, behind her tinted spectacles, he could discern an oriental aspect to her eyes.

She turned back to Damian, "I've a complicated heart problem, and I think I'm going to have to have quite a major operation: a transplant, or something. I'd been hoping to go home to visit some of my relatives before I got worse, but I don't think that's going to be possible." She was clearly glad to have someone with whom to talk, although Damian was so much younger. He nevertheless had a sympathetic and compassionate manner.

"Are your relatives far away?" he asked.

"They could hardly be further – the Philippines." She replied. She paused, "I almost got to the point of booking the flight," she added, "but then I realised that I wouldn't be able to manage such a long journey."

"I was thinking of going to the Philippines – to Naga City," burst out Damian, and he went on to recount briefly what Father Chris had suggested.

45

At that moment, the receptionist called out "Mrs Smith to see Doctor Farthing" and the little oriental lady got up and disappeared into the surgery. Fifteen minutes elapsed before she returned to the waiting room, went up to Damian and said, "Look, here's my address and phone number." She handed him a card. "If you decide to go to the Philippines I would be very grateful if you'd take a small parcel to my family there. I didn't have the opportunity to say when the Doctor called for me just now, that they all live in Naga City. And," she added, "I'm more than happy to pay for your fare out there."

At that point the receptionist came in again and called "Mr Damian Debden." He uttered a quick and bewildered, "Thank you," entered the surgery whilst Mrs Smith disappeared out of the main door.

Later that morning, with the eczema suitably treated, Damian reflected on his conversation with the lady in the doctor's waiting room. It really had been an extraordinary encounter and an even more extraordinary offer made to him. He had certainly prayed about it as Father Chris had enjoined and this seemed to be the answer to his prayer.

The following day he took out the card Mrs Smith had given him. She lived not far from him in Shepherds Bush. He decided to phone her. Yes, she had meant what she had said, and she was delighted that she could be of help.

"I just want you to call on my sister in Naga city and give her the small parcel I'll let you have. Maybe you could call on me tomorrow morning and I'll give it to you together with enough money for the airfare. Meanwhile you could check out the times of flights."

Damian complied with her request, decided on a possible flight via Bangkok where he would have to change for Manila, and then went to see Mrs Smith still hardly believing that it could all be true. He was greeted very warmly and she insisted on his consuming various small sweet delicacies clearly of a Philippine origin.

"Yes, I make them myself," she said.

She then gave him the parcel which was not large, but fairly heavy and addressed to a Mrs Holland.

"I need to know what's in it," said Damian, "as I may be asked at the check-in or by customs the other end."

"Yes, of course, and I'll tell you. There are two quite valuable volumes of the old 'Strand Magazine' published at the end of the nineteenth century which contain the original Sherlock Holmes stories, and then there's a third book of family photos and some letters all of which will be of great interest to my sister's grandchildren. I won't need them any more. The time I have on this earth is not long now and I do want the family to have them before I die. You will be rendering me a very great service by taking them."

So it was that just five days later Damian met Father Chris at the airport. He had already phoned him and related his unexpected encounter in the doctor's surgery.

"You see," Chris had said, "it is clearly God's will that you go there. That's the way the Lord works." Before bidding Father Chris farewell and thanking him, Damian said,

"You know, Father, you've still not told me anything about Eziat."

"You'll hear something about it from the brothers in the Philippines and for the rest, you'll have to wait until you return." With that Damian passed through the security checks and on to the departure gate.

Naga City, Damian's destination, was on the same main island as Manila, the capital. It was one of nearly eight thousand islands which comprised the Philippines. He read something about it from a magazine he found on the plane. However, on several occasions during the flight his thoughts went back to Shirley and he wondered how she was feeling now. He had written to her, briefly, to tell her of his immediate plans but she had not replied. "Well, perhaps that was just as well," he thought. He purposely had not phoned as he thought she, and probably he as well, would become too emotional.

Anyway, he had to draw a line under all that. In future he would write at Christmas and for her birthday; and no doubt she would soon meet someone else and marry.

Father Chris had arranged for him to be met at Manila by one of the Brothers, and as he came through the Arrivals barrier at the airport terminal he immediately espied a white habited figure with a blue sash. Damian went towards him and introduced himself.

"And I'm Brother Bernard," the other answered. He was probably about 30 years of age and looked Indian. "You are very welcome and we are delighted to meet you." He led Damian to a dirty old red car parked outside the terminal. It was just after six o'clock, rush hour time in the evening, and already getting dark when they drove off, weaving in and out of the crowded streets. Damian noticed that the main trunk roads were quite narrow with only a single lane in each direction. Vehicles frequently had no rear lights and often only one front light which could be on either the right or the left or occasionally even in the middle, and very few seemed ever to dip their headlights, including Bernard, who clearly conformed to the local customs.

There were many hazards on the road not least being the pedalled or motorised tricycles carrying anything up to three or four people in a tiny side-carriage; and then there were the colourful jeepneys which were like mini-buses intended for about fifteen people but often carrying twice that number. Most of them had inadequate lighting and after overtaking two of them, a third would suddenly appear from the right with an oncoming coach charging towards them on the left. Damian would close his eyes waiting for the expected smash and crunch as they would surely be squeezed between the two vehicles. However, somehow it was avoided and they pressed on until they arrived just beyond the suburbs of Manila and Bernard announced that they were nearly out of gas. The American terminology was used for petrol; this was due to the influence of the American occupation of the Philippines.

"You know," remarked Bernard, who was chatting away continually, steering the car being a secondary occupation, "In Mindanao in the south of the Philippines, the Americans are recorded as opportunists but here in the north they're an opportunity. We could hardly do without them."

They pulled in at what was apparently the last service station for the next hundred kilometres and Bernard commented that he had not eaten since breakfast, so perhaps they could buy a sandwich at McDonald's which adjoined the petrol station. Having fed both bodies and vehicle, they resumed their journey south eastward along a bumpy road which scarcely allowed room for the oncoming traffic to pass. Most of the way this included many heavy lorries. Bernard seemed attracted to the idea of overtaking a lorry on his side of the road only when he saw another one advancing towards them on the other side. Headlights flashed, horns sounded and once again Damian closed his eyes.

After a further four hours on the road, Damian who was occasionally responding to remarks by Bernard and partly dozing off, asked "Are they the lights of Naga ahead of us". "Oh No", replied Brother Bernard , "We're only about halfway there yet ". In parts the road became pot holed and rough and the car did much swerving and turning to avoid the holes as well as oncoming traffic. Damian imagined that in daylight the scenery would be spectacular as he could just discern the dark shapes of hills and trees.

Finally at three o clock in the morning they arrived at their destination and bed, somewhat hard and forbidding, nevertheless beckoned. Later in the morning partly refreshed, Damian took stock of his surroundings. He had slept at one end of a dormitory containing fifty bunk beds, some with mosquito nets. His had been equipped with one, but in the dark and with his need of sleep he had failed to make use of it. Fortunately none of these malicious two-winged female insects had attacked him. He had missed breakfast but one of the brothers gave him some water, dry bread and fruit during which he learned that the community had been there for the past ten years and that they ran a centre for the mentally and physically disabled and homeless. There were ten Brothers , most of them from the Philippines, a few of them being under training, but all had some sort of involvement with looking after the poor.

Their centre was situated on the edge of a vast conglomeration of squatter dwellings. Around them wild life, frogs, birds and snakes, as well as turtles, dogs, hens and sheep, flourished amongst the mixed vegetation of bamboos, banana trees, coconut palms and rice fields. The centre provided a home for well over a hundred disabled people, mostly children and the elderly.

Damian was shown around by one of the brothers and met many of the squatters living in the nearby shanty town. Not far away was an enormous rubbish dump on the edge of which twenty seven families lived in a small huddle of makeshift huts. These were mostly built of odd pieces of wood, corrugated iron, matting and other materials all somehow pieced together. Rubbish and garbage were piled high around them and between the huts were blackened dirt paths, many of which had small pieces of broken glass embedded in them. Bare footed children played in the dirt and Damian was told that each tiny one-roomed dwelling would house a whole family, which would mean probably parents with six or seven children.

The father of the family would spend the daylight hours searching amongst the rubbish for anything that could be salvaged. One man was collecting dirty used plastic beakers which he hoped to sell for recycling. There was an old fashioned pump near the main road on the edge of the site and this was the only water supply for all the families, the toilet being a hole in the ground.

The women spent much of their time gathered in or around a central hut which had a small make-shift altar at one end and a few chairs. They would often take part in bible-study led by a nun who came in from Naga. With nothing, or at least very little, of this world's goods, their faith was nevertheless strong, and the highlight of their week was when one of the Brothers, a priest, came to celebrate the Sunday Mass in the central hut. He told Damian that it was the highlight of his week too.

Most of the families had lived there for several years and the children knew no other way of life. Many of them would go with their father onto the garbage and join him in scavenging. This was not only a highly unhealthy occupation, but it could be dangerous. Just a short while back a small child had been accidentally scooped up by a digger and killed.

One day Damian was taken to a state controlled local mental hospital. Two of the brothers would visit the inmates twice a week. For Damian it turned out to be one of the most traumatic experiences of his life.

There were two main single storey buildings in the hospital, one for men and the other for women. A veranda ran alongside the men's section and giving on to this were four dimly lit rooms. The floors were concrete, but Damian was told that until recently they had been just mud. About four feet from the ground there were long horizontal barred openings letting in a little light and air. The doors to each room were heavily barred and bolted.

As the two brothers approached with Damian, bare arms and hands pushed through the spaces between the bars and faces appeared demanding recognition. Damian found a gap to look beyond the arms and heads to what was in the room. Inside the largest of them, which was an area of about twenty by ten metres, all he could see was a completely open area devoid of any furniture and over the rough concrete floor there were a few dirty mats and pieces of board between which were pools of liquid which, judging by the smell, was urine. In one corner a low wall about a meter high enclosed a two metre square area with a hole in the floor and a water tap. This was the toilet and wash place for the thirty-four men who lived all their days and nights in the place. Food would be passed through a gap beneath the iron door. Most of the men in all four rooms were completely naked, others wore just a dirty pair of underpants or shorts.

One young man, about 25 years of age, clasped Damian's hand through the bars and exclaimed, "You're from London! I was at Heathrow three years ago! You know Heathrow?"

Others pushed their way forward squeezing the first person against the bars. All wanted to touch Damian and speak with him and were calling out to be heard.

All self-respect was absent and Damian decided that animals were treated far better than these men.

On each occasion when the Brothers visited, a few of the inmates would be allowed out on to the verandah where they could have their nails and hair cut and given a good shower. Damian joined in this work, and whilst doing so, discovered that a few had been seminarians studying for the priesthood. "What had gone wrong?" he enquired. It appeared that their families had to pay for their training and after a year or two could no longer afford it.

The young men would then become depressed and might turn to the compensation of drugs, drink or sex. This resulted in a mental breakdown and, because their families would feel the disgrace of this – "What will our friends and neighbours think?" – he would be abandoned and end up in this state mental institution.

The women's section, Damian found, was similar, although not quite as dark and dreary. Some Religious Sisters regularly visited the women, some of whom were also naked, but several had a basic iron bedstead to lie on, but no mattress.

Some of the residents looked after by the Brothers in their Centre had formerly been living in this mental hospital, but now they were being properly cared for, clean, adequately clothed, well fed and treated with dignity and respect.

For Damian the days passed quickly and it was only after having been with the Brothers for some weeks that he found an opportunity to go into the town and find the address that Mrs Smith had given him. He eventually located the street and found the front-door of the house sandwiched inconspicuously between a shop and what seemed to be a derelict shattered building. There was no knocker or bell so he banged on the door which was almost immediately opened by a lady whose features resembled those of Mrs Smith. This must be the sister, he thought, and he was about to introduce himself when the lady in question said immediately,

"You must be Damian Debden, the young man my sister phoned me about. Come in! You are most welcome. Come in!" she repeated The front door opened into a surprisingly spacious room, one part of which was arranged with comfortable chairs and coffee tables, whilst further in Damian saw a large round table set for a meal for some eight or nine people.

"Sit down. I am Rose, Rose Holland. I am Alice Smith's sister as you probably realise and she told me something about you and it's great to meet you", she paused for a moment. "Is she very ill? How does she look?"

Damian tried to answer those questions as discreetly and as tactfully as possible. Then, after a few more questions, several other members of the family came and in and were introduced to Damian. All seemed to want to ask question after question about London and what it was really like there. Meanwhile, several of the family were rapidly loading the table with a variety of dishes. They persuaded Damian to join them for the meal and when they were eventually all seated, they prayed for a moment before Mrs Holland carefully explained to Damian what each dish contained.

There were reyenong bangus, a sort of milky fish, adobong manok, chicken and baboy, pork. There was also isda, which he was told was sweet and sour fish, other meat dishes, vegetables, salads and various desserts. It was overwhelming as he was persuaded to taste everything and it was a very different menu from what he had experienced at table in the Brothers' community.

The conversation moved from questions about England, and London, to a discussion about the state of the world, and about America in particular. It seemed that most Philippinos were pro-American, probably because that was where, in a sense, lay their bread and butter. Damian recalled that for nearly fifty years the country had been taken over from the Spanish by the Americans and had not become independent until 1946. Most people had a slight American accent.

The weeks and months passed quickly and for nearly a year Damian stayed helping the Brothers in their very full regime of prayer and work with the poor and homeless. He was saddened at the thought of returning to England. He had corresponded just three times with Shirley and, in her last letter, he was relieved to learn that she was friendly with someone she had met in the library where she had been working. He felt once again liberated, although it somehow challenged him to think further about what decision he had to take after his return. Did he still feel the call of the priesthood?

For the moment his attention was entirely taken up with preparing for the moment of his departure from the people he had been helping each day, the families on the rubbish dump, the patients in the mental hospital, and perhaps, most of all, the small community of Brothers with whom he had lived and shared so happily and joyfully over the past months. Finally, the sad moment of farewell came, and just before Brother Bernard dropped him off at the airport he said, "Damian, don't forget to call on our community at Eziat and give them our love and assure them that we are united in our prayer each day, and," he added, "a special greeting to Father Chris." A few days after Damian's return he called up Father Chris who immediately said, "Yes, come and see me tomorrow morning. I'll be at Eziat. You've not been there yet, but you'll find it easily: it's just walking distance from Epping, the last station on the Central Line."

Chapter 4 – Arcane?

Gordon Greenford was clad in shorts as it was a warm June day and he was setting out on a cycling holiday. He felt the usual sensations of excitement and anticipation and was reminded of the Mole in "The Wind in the Willows" who abandoned his spring-cleaning, and with the call of the open-air burrowed up to the surface and began his adventures with his new-found friend the Rat. Kenneth Grahame's book had always been one of Gordon's favourites as a child and even now as an adult.

Gordon was going to meet, not a new-found friend, but Andrew, someone who had also completed his second year at university and whom he had known since their school days together. Gordon's mother had seen him off from their home in Ruislip. His father, a doctor, was already on duty at his surgery in Acton.

Gordon got on the Central Line to go to Queensway where Andrew lived. It was the morning rush hour and he thought again of the Mole who had considered that the best part of a holiday was perhaps not so much to be resting yourself as to see all the other fellows busy working.

However, he encountered his first set-back – he was to have others later – when his train was held up in the tunnel just short of the Queensway underground station. Fortunately, it was not a long delay, but with the necessary diversion he eventually arrived at Andrew's house three-quarters of an hour after their agreed rendezvous time.

Andrew, who was studying engineering, was the more practical of the two and he had been fixing new brakes on Gordon's bicycle. All was now ready, and the two cycles were loaded and Andrew's mother, an inveterate worrier, was standing at the door issuing a string of parental warnings. These ranged from concerns about traffic, people they might meet, damp clothes, sufficient food and various items they may have forgotten to include in their luggage. Andrew tried to remonstrate with his mother: "We are both adult, Mum, so you don't need to worry!"

At last they were away, relieved at being able to escape from the home chains.

Andrew understood why his mother was so protective, even though he was now twenty years of age. She was widowed after only nine years of married life when her husband was away in Brussels on business – he was a civil engineer – and on returning to London his plane had crashed and there had been no survivors. His wife, Sonia, was left with two children, Andrew and his sister Becky who was just two years older. She had left school at eighteen and gone to a dancing academy. Walking home one night the short distance from the bus to the house in Ealing, a drunken driver had mounted the pavement and crushed her against the wall of a house. She had multiple injuries, from most of which she had recovered, but the worst outcome had been a partial paralysis in her legs which meant that she could walk only with difficulty and usually with two sticks. Sonia had found this second tragedy harder to accept than Becky herself, and one result was that she had become over-protective and possessive of both Becky and Andrew.

Becky was living in a nearby flat with a girl friend, but Andrew usually spent his university vacations at home with his mother.

Gordon's mother, Alice, also had a strong personality, but this was softened by the presence of her husband. His kindly doctor's bedside manner was sometimes seen to be useful in the home. Alice clearly tried not to spoil her son but it was inevitable that Gordon benefited materially through not having brothers and sisters with whom to share. He was through with his second year at University reading English, but he was uncertain what he would do after he, hopefully, qualified. Perhaps he would teach. Both Gordon and Andrew were interested in architecture and ancient buildings and with this in mind they had planned their holiday to include Oxford and then to cycle northwards to explore some of the ruined abbeys of Yorkshire.

Once away from home, they eventually escaped also from the congested and polluted area of the London suburbs and the home counties and approached the sweeping meadows and trees of the Chilterns until they were down near the Thames beyond Henley. The road had levelled out and they had decided to spend their first night near Oxford.

Just as they came to the village of Dorchester, a heavy shower of rain descended on them. It was clearly the moment to stop and Andrew, who was always keen on exploring old buildings, suggested sheltering in the ancient abbey church which stood conveniently a few yards away. As they stood their bikes against the stone wall of the church, their attention was drawn to a fairy tale white and black-beamed cottage nestling near the tombstones which surrounded the abbey.

The abbey was, at that time, in need of repair, but it was nevertheless an imposingly severe and solemn structure dating from the twelfth century when it had replaced two earlier Saxon cathedrals. Just as Andrew was about to read more from the notice in the porch, an old woman came from the cottage and greeted them.

"D'you want to 'ave a look inside?" she asked in a typical Oxfordshire accent. She had long white hair which hung in straight-clusters from around the crown of her head which was almost bald. There was something strange in her personal appearance and the continued movement of her eyes – first to Andrew, then to Gordon and then to the door of the church and on to one of the nearby tombs near the entrance.

"Thanks," replied Andrew.

"Y'erve no doubt come to see the Jesse window, I suppose" added the old lady.

"Well, yes, we would like to see it" said Andrew, implying that he already knew quite a bit about it, although it was the first time he'd heard of it.

"There it is," said the old woman, and as they entered, she pointed to over the left of the chancel. At that, without a further word, she disappeared back through the door just as a figure appeared from the door into the bell tower. "Ah, come to see the Jesse window, have you?" It was a man in a shabby grey suit, thick rimmed spectacles and a clerical collar that had slipped slightly from its anchorage.

"There it is, over there," and he pointed in the same direction that had been indicated by the woman.

"Thanks," said Andrew, "and can we have a general look around, and take a few photos?"

"Of course, of course. It's a wonderful church, full of interest. There's a guide book you can read. Can't give you any time myself: must be off to catch that old lady before she runs off. She's my housekeeper and is becoming senile, poor soul."

Gordon and Andrew were left on their own in the church. Andrew, whose enthusiasm for architecture was greater than Gordon's, soon was happily taking photos until he came close up to the Jesse window. They both looked closely at the fourteenth century stained glass characters framed beautifully by the carved stone branches of the Jesse tree. In this were portrayed other antecedents of Christ, each one seeming to vie for attention competing with those represented in the glass. Some of the figures had been restored after being smashed by Cromwell's men.

However, there was one figure in the bottom right-hand corner of the window which caught Gordon's attention. It was King David, the son of Jesse, who lay at the base and from whom the tree sprang, apparently having escaped the Cromwellian onslaught on religious imagery. He was playing the harp and a gleam of afternoon sunshine coming from the other side of the abbey caught his crown and seemed to move on to the harp. His head was tilted and, as Gordon looked, he seemed to move. His head was looking up and across and viewing the other figures in the window. "It must be my imagination," thought Gordon. Perhaps they'd cycled too far for one day and he was suffering from hunger and thirst and this has caused some sort of hallucination. He looked again and called to Andrew.

They both looked. Andrew said that he saw nothing unusual and moved away again. Gordon, however, was sure that David was no longer gazing across at the figures level with him. He was moving slowly, moving towards first one and then another. By this time Andrew had disappeared to view the exterior of the grey stone abbey.

When Gordon looked again, it seemed as though a sudden flash of light enveloped all the characters in the window and he thought he heard David's voice speaking in turn to each of the characters in that genealogy, springing from the root of Jesse and extending at the top of the window to Christ himself.

The stone carved image of David seemed to move from one figure to another, from stained glass to stone statues, from an antecedent to a descendant, from a damaged face to one that was clearly identifiable.

Always it was the same phrase. Gordon could hear it quite clearly. "The Lord is compassion and love." "The Lord is compassion and love." "The Lord is compassion and love."

Then David seemed to return to his place on the right hand bottom corner of the window, still uttering that phrase. Then he seemed to turn to Gordon. But no, it could not be: perhaps this was some strange game that the vicar played on unwary visitors? Yes, that was it. It could hardly be otherwise.

By this time David had turned and seemed to be looking directly at Gordon from the corner of the window. He was no longer saying, "The Lord is compassion and love," but Gordon now heard him saying, "Look at my life. You know God really is compassion and love. When I was a young man I had a great friend Jonathan. We were very close. We did everything together. I really loved Jonathan. Then my way of life changed and, to my shame, I committed adultery. I know, in those days, you could have a number of wives, but it was against the law to steal another person's wife. And that's what I did.

I saw Bathsheba bathing naked, and she was so attractive. Just before she finished she looked up and I think she saw me looking at her from the palace roof. I was carried away. I went to see her and the inevitable happened. We had intercourse. Her husband Uriah, an officer in the army, was away in the army at the time.

A few weeks later she sent a message to me saying that she was pregnant. What was I to do as Uriah hadn't had leave for some months? I sent orders for him to come home on leave but the silly fellow had decided not to lie with his wife until after the battle he was engaged in had been won. There was only one way out of the problem. I sent orders that he should be in the front line, where he'd almost certainly be killed. Then life would be simple, Bathsheba could join the rest of my wives.

Well, Uriah was killed, just as I'd planned. I had to wait a while for Bathsheba to go through the regulation time of mourning, but then I had her as my wife, and everything went smoothly for a while, except that from time to time my conscience got in the way of my peace of mind.

There was a good and holy man whom I was acquainted with, just slightly, and one day he came to see me and told me a story about a rich man who had lots of sheep, but went to steal the one and only sheep owned by a poor man. This wise man, Nathan, made me realise that I had acted in a similar way, only much worse. It shook me to the depths of my being and I realised how despicably I'd acted.

Bathsheba's baby was born – my baby too – but it was delicate and frail, and soon became quite ill and died. I did my best to comfort Bathsheba. She then had another child. This time all was well, and eventually, after many years had passed this second son, Solomon, took over from me as King.

However, in the meantime I had had several problems with other children by some of my other wives: Absolom for one. He killed his half-brother, Ammon, and then ran off. But, worse than that, he started to plot against me and I was forced to leave Jerusalem and, with a great crowd of supporters, fight against Absolom. Of course, he really wanted to be king himself. He was a good-looking, proud and ambitious young man.

There was a lot of fighting and many were killed, both my own men and Absolom's. In the end Absolom had to admit defeat and he turned away from the scene of battle and rode into a nearby forest.

Then a tragic thing occurred. He didn't notice a branch of a tree overhanging the path and he rode straight into it and became hooked onto it by the neck of his armour. I don't know how long he hung there. His horse travelled on and away. But then Joab, the commander of my army came along and decided that the half-completed task of the tree should be completed, and he thrust a spear through Absolom's body.

When I heard the news, I suppose I was in some way relieved, but also very distressed. After all, Absolom was my son, my own flesh and blood. He wasn't the only one of my sons who wanted to succeed me. There were several others with that sole aim in life. Adonijah was one. Oh, the troubles I had. But I knew all the time that Bathsheba's son, Solomon, was to take over from me. God brought good out of all my mistakes and the bad things I did; and I suppose, gradually, by the end of those forty years on the throne, I really learned that "the Lord is compassion and love." I deliberately caused the death of someone; I experienced the appalling death of my son Absolom; I was proud and cruel and broke the commandments, and yet the Messiah chose to be born of my descendants. He came from the line of David, my line, my family. I still find that quite extraordinary and humiliating.

Yes, I wrote that psalm because it was a sort of echo of so much that had happened in my life. Well, that's my story. What about you?"

The words failed to register at first. Then Gordon realised that it was the same voice uttering the question. That strange vicar must have set off a recording. What was he saying?

"What about you?" came the question again. This time Gordon was sure that it was directed to him. What really was happening? Was he experiencing a remarkable vision of heavenly things? Was it all in his imagination? It could be. Then again he heard the question. This time it went on, "What about you, how do you see your life? Are you as close to your friend, Andrew, as I was to Jonathan"?

This last question shook him a little. He was very fond of Andrew. They would not have agreed to holiday together if this had not been true. However, they had never talked about their relationship and no advances had been made by either of them. Being gay was spoken of openly. Gordon's thoughts then turned to his "students", the young men who, in his mid-teen imaginary world, he used to talk with and teach. He had never spoken of them to anyone at all. There was 'David' who was prominent in the Group, and on whom he leaned and asked for help and advice and shared his thoughts and problems. These imaginary beings had been real to Gordon for the past six years. They were all of another world and perhaps came into this imaginary existence because of a loneliness and isolation that he felt through not having any brothers and sisters.

His thoughts then turned to what seemed to be happening in this vast empty old church. Was it haunted? And then he suddenly thought; where was Andrew? He hadn't seen him for a while.

It seemed a long time whilst David was speaking. Had Andrew, whom Gordon trusted, nevertheless decided to play a game with him? But how could that be possible? Even had he been just outside the Jesse window, surely in no way could he have been the cause of what Gordon had experienced.

As these puzzled thoughts were flooding through his mind he became aware of a figure in black standing in the corner of the chapel near the tombs. Was it the vicar? It didn't look quite like him, and yet as the figure moved towards Gordon he realised it was the vicar. "Ah, you've been studying the Jesse window," he remarked.

"Er, yes," answered Gordon a little nervously.

"It's a very extraordinary window," remarked the man in black. Some people see more in it than first meets the eye."

"Yes," said Gordon somewhat meekly.

"They imagine," he continued, "that one of the figures is speaking to them and advising them. I've never seen anything extraordinary in it myself, except, of course, its uniqueness and its unusual beauty." He paused. "Do you like it?" He shot this last question at Gordon suddenly.

After a moment's hesitation Gordon answered him, "I thought I saw the figure of King David move......And then he seemed to speak," he added.

"Many say that. Did you hear what he said?" asked the vicar.

"Yes - the Lord is compassion and love. I think that is from one of the psalms."

"That's not what he says to some of the other visitors. I think you should take that quite personally, especially for yourself – a special message. Keep it as your particular motto, if you like."

"Did you cause the movement and sounds?" Gordon plucked up courage to ask him.

He evaded the question. "Yes, it's a strange old window, and sometimes, you know, through ancient relics of bygone ages we become linked with, even communicate with, people and events of the past. Don't ask me how it happens. Maybe there's something in you that resonates with a quality or weakness, or characteristic found in King David, although he lived a very long time ago."

"Perhaps," said Gordon. "Anyway," he quickly went on, "I must go and find my friend as we have to get to Oxford before it's too late. Thank you for your help."

Gordon hastened out of the abbey, still unsure whether the black-clothed man really was the vicar with whom he had been speaking, and even more unsure as to whether he had been playing a strange sort of joke on him.

Andrew was still looking around outside, but they were both anxious to move on to Oxford, so Gordon didn't recount to him his experiences until later that night. They were both tired by then, and Andrew just brushed it all off as a recording devised by the vicar. Perhaps it was.

However, the words of King David stuck in Gordon's mind. He also wondered if there was a connection between the David of his imagination and what he had been experiencing of the Old Testament David.

Over the next few days little else of interest occurred, and after exploring some of the wonders of Oxford they turned northwards, heading for Yorkshire.

Just before nightfall one day, they arrived at a Youth Hostel a few miles from their destination, Fountains Abbey, the most interesting of the ruined abbeys in that part of the country. The warden of the hostel was a Mrs Dooley and she turned out to be a friendly soul, so much so that she persuaded Andrew and Gordon and two other hostellers, "the love birds" as Mrs Dooley called them, together with Trudy her spaniel, to walk down to the local after supper.

The publican's wife, a strangely quiet woman whose girth was as great as her height, served the beer, and Andrew and Gordon stood Mrs Dooley a drink. The young lovers soon left to continue their perambulations alone. Their exit prompted a few caustic and unrepeatable remarks from Mrs Dooley. It is true that the girl was wearing an absurdly short skirt!

Mrs Dooley was an extremely jolly person. Her husband had contracted an illness and was selling the cycle shop he owned in Hull and they were both going to the south of France later in the year. Her dog, Trudy, caused some amusement, for it was scratching, noisily and frequently. Mrs Dooley, on seeing Andrew contemplating the itching animal, remarked, "I really think she scratches for the sake of scratching!"

To which he could not refrain from adding "We hope so!"

Whereupon, while still on the subject of dogs, Mrs Dooley related the story of a friend of hers who gave her dog rum and it became so drunk that it fell over every time it tried to put its leg up!

The next day they were up and enthusiastic to visit Fountains Abbey. This, so Gordon had previously read, was "the crown and glory of all that monasticism has left to us in England." It all began when thirteen monks from the Benedictine Abbey of St Mary in York wanted to lead a stricter life and so they left York and moved to Skelldale which was described as "a place which had never been inhabited, overgrown with thorns, a hollow in the hills between projecting rocks; fitter to all appearance, to be a lair of wild beasts than a home for men!" At first the rocks were literally their only shelter, but soon they chose a great elm in the middle of the valley, and thatched a sort of hut around its trunk. At first these poor monks, vowed to poverty, obedience to the Abbot Richard whom they had elected, and chastity, could in no way imagine the great edifice that was soon to rise on the spot. Their daily work consisted in making mats, cutting faggots to construct a wattled oratory, whilst some took to cultivating the ground.

They agreed to follow the stricter rule of the Cistercians founded by St Bernard in Clairvaux.

Their numbers increased, money flowed in, more land was donated and extensive building was embarked on. The increased prosperity later led to a decline in the spiritual tone of the monastery until, in 1539, the buildings were surrendered to Henry VIII, the monks dispersed, and the enormous revenues from well over 60,000 acres of land, more than 200 cattle and sheep, to say nothing of the gold and silver from the church, went to fill the royal coffers. King Henry was badly in need of money for his campaign against Spain.

Gordon was sharing some of these details with Andrew as they parked their bicycles near the gate and walked along the path bordering the small river Skell. Happily, Andrew thought, there seemed to be no other visitors. It was still only ten o'clock in the morning. Together they explored the various remaining parts of the monastery and surroundings. At least here, Gordon thought, there were no statues to talk to him.

Andrew was the more interested of the two in the style of architecture and he was noticing the strange combination of the twenty two pointed nave arches with the round Norman arches and windows of the bays. They both stood beneath the great tower which, although built much later than the rest, was still in the purer Gothic style, as if Abbot Huby who was responsible for it had a nostalgia for the past. It was at that moment, whilst looking up at the tower from the middle of the nave, that a strange almost inhuman sound came from the direction of what had been the infirmary which led off from the chapel of nine altars to the east.

Gordon heard the sound and he immediately looked at Andrew. Had he also heard it or was this another strange experience like that at Dorchester? Yes, Gordon was relieved to hear Andrew saying, "Did you hear that? What was it?" It was a sound as of a high-pitched moaning of someone in pain.

"It came from over there," replied Gordon pointing towards the nine altars' chapel "-through that opening," and he started moving in that direction. They walked through the chapel and further over the to the east and then they both saw an extraordinary light. Just inside the entrance to what had been the infirmary was a simple wooden bedstead with a dark brown blanket partly covering a man with an emaciated face, a brown hood pulled over his head and as they looked at him, bewildered and fearful, he cried out "Ora, ora pro me..." and with one further high-pitched moaning cry he vanished. He was no longer there. There was no sign of him anywhere.

"Gosh," exclaimed Andrew, "We've seen a ghost. I didn't really think they existed," he added, "but we both saw it, didn't we? Wasn't it extraordinary – and weird?"

"That's my second strange experience in a few days," said Gordon. "This could hardly be the product of our imagination as we both saw and heard exactly the same thing. There's no one else around here: no other visitors."

"What was he trying to say?" asked Andrew.

"I think it was Latin," said Gordon. "'Ora' means 'pray' – pray for me. That must have been it. Catholics pray for the dead. He must have been the ghost of a dead monk and he wanted us to pray for him."

"I'm not sure that I understand that," said Andrew.

"Well, Catholics believe," said Gordon who seemed to know something about it although he wasn't a Catholic, "that when you die you have to go through a final stage of purification, called purgatory, in order to be ready for life with God in heaven; and we can help souls who've died with our prayers whilst they're in that state."

"Yes, I see that, but I can't quite see how it works because I thought that time only exists here in this life so why go on praying to God for someone who died a long time ago? Seems a bit odd to me."

"Yes, it is mysterious. I'm really going on what I've read. I can't say I believe it or understand it. I suppose," he continued slowly, "the nearest you can get to thinking of eternity or timelessness is to think of times when you're tremendously happy with someone you love or doing something you like doing, then you're just not aware of time. A day can seem like a few minutes."

"Gosh, that sounds very expert for someone who isn't a Christian and I must say you seem to know a lot about it. I didn't know you were so interested in religion. That dream, or whatever it was that you had at Dorchester, must have affected you."

"Well, perhaps," said Gordon, "but we've both experienced the same thing here at Fountains, haven't we?"

"I'm really not sure – of anything," replied Andrew, "except, of course," he added smiling, "constructing buildings and bridges. That's something I can be sure about. Anyway, what do you think about ghosts? How do they fit into the scheme of things?"

"I don't really know anything, except what I've read." He then went on to expound on the subject, "There are different explanations of ghosts," he continued, "Some places really are haunted and the spirits of the dead can influence material things. Science, after all, tells us that matter can be converted into energy and vice versa. It's a sort of transformation of energy and matter. I suppose, sometimes, it could also be an expression of someone's subconscious." Here Gordon was wondering whether this would explain the mysterious experience he'd had at Dorchester.

Andrew listened attentively. By this time they had both seated themselves on a nearby bench and were facing towards the beautiful and serene stone ruins of Fountains.

"I can understand and accept the existence of telepathy, the transference of thoughts and ideas from one person to another, but what you're saying is more difficult to appreciate. Could it not be just a vivid imagination?" And then he immediately added, "That might explain your Dorchester experience but not what we've both just seen here. Gosh, it's puzzling!" he exclaimed.

At that point a group of not very quiet school children in their mid-teens arrived with two male teachers who seemed to have little control over them and the silence was shattered. Andrew and Gordon decided to leave. They were hoping, anyway, to head southwards and within two days fairly hard cycling, avoiding most of the main roads, to reach London and home.

They set off, but they were destined to have one more strange encounter before they arrived at their respective homes.

It was the afternoon of the following day and they had stopped just near the tiny village of Stilton, where the cheese of that name originates, at the beginning of a quiet country lane and were enjoying a light snack before hopefully reaching Huntingdon for the night. Suddenly, from a few feet away and seemingly from the depth of the hedgerow came a deep and loud voice with a pronounced Irish accent, "Hail young men! You've the chance to meet the Pilgrim-Poet, and I greet you both with great joy!"

At that, the owner of the voice appeared in a gap in the hedge. He was a tall man with a long tangled grey beard, reddish grey hair and twinkling blue eyes.

"Meet Francis Buckhurst-Hill, a traveller of the open roads of Europe, originally from County Mayo in the holy land of Ireland. At this he strode up to Gordon and Andrew and burst into song:

O land of joy and beauty
Where shamrock holds the sway,
And Tinkers fight with madness
Whilst Tramps sleep out in hay;
Thy land has many wondrous charms,
To please the weary eyes,
But there are some who really try
Thy freedom to despise.
O land of faith and legend,
In this world oft, are few
Who carry out the works of Christ,
Some seldom really do;
If all but sought to serve him,
This world could surely be,
A land of saints and scholars,
And joyful harmony.
O pray for me dear Ireland,
And all thy beggars too!

Who roam about from town to town,
But holy men are few;
Alas this world is weary,
Of sin beyond repair,
Except by meditation,
On love beyond compare.

"And that's my elegy to Ireland," he stated in conclusion.

He had a good deep bass voice, which combined with the Irish accent created a picture of green glens, grass-covered slopes and grey stone walls.

"You've a great voice," said Andrew. "Thank you for that song. We've not been to Ireland, but perhaps one day we will."

"Yes, keep travelling. Keep moving. I never stay anywhere for long. The longest was three months in a mental hospital after getting knocked down by a car and having a broken arm – the left one. I didn't know what they were trying to repair – my mind or my arm. Ah well, I must move on now before nightfall. Good to have met you both."

At that he gathered up a dirty haversack which had been hidden under the hedge and a rustic stick which he swung in the air as he marched off, humming the tune he'd already sung.

"What a character," exclaimed Gordon. "I thought he was going to ask us for money, but he seemed a really genuine tramp. He was real enough and certainly no ghost."

Shortly after the third strange encounter, they cycled through the northern suburbs of London, arriving at the end of what they agreed was a worthwhile tour of parts of

England. Soon their studies called and, although their friendship continued, they were unable to spend much time together. Communication continued, mostly, by means of e-mail.

Both of them qualified in their final exams with flying colours. Gordon was accepted for a post in a secondary school in the Docklands area of London, teaching English to multi-cultural classes of youngsters, mostly the products of broken homes. It was not easy.

Andrew was employed by an engineering firm and was asked to work on a road bridge over a river running into the Bosphorus. He was given a flat in Istanbul.

Thus it was, that one day Gordon was delighted to receive an e-mail from Andrew inviting him for a fortnight's holiday in Turkey. Andrew would arrange it all to coincide with school holidays and Gordon had only to book his flight. On the day of Gordon's departure he reflected on their previous holiday cycling in Oxfordshire and Yorkshire. This was going to be very different and without the semi-mystical experiences they'd had previously. However, in this he was mistaken.

He greatly looked forward to seeing Andrew again, to sharing many of his thoughts and feelings, yes, and fears that he was experiencing in his teaching. He looked forward to the warm and prolonged hug they would greet each other with. This could be misinterpreted by an onlooker. However, neither could be described as gay. They were both attracted to the opposite sex although neither had as yet met "the right one".

Friendship was important to them both. When they were together there was the desire at times to be away from other people, and yet neither indulged in erotic thoughts about the other. Their friendship, indeed one could say their love for each other, was platonic. When together they shared many of their innermost thoughts and responded to events with a similar laid-back humour.

And so it was that when Gordon came through the arrivals barrier at Istanbul Attaturk airport and saw Andrew waiting for him a smile and a great hug was the order of the day.

"It's really great to see you, Gordon," Andrew greeted him.

"Yes, that goes for me, too," responded Gordon. "We've a lot to talk about."

"And I've got great plans for our time together," added Andrew.

They made their way by bus and foot to Andrew's flat which was well within the bounds of the city. For Gordon it was a strange and intriguing introduction to a very different culture. Noise seemed to invade every possible crevice and resonate between buildings either side of the narrow streets. This, he found later, was regularly punctuated by the sound of the muezzin five times a day, although the first seemed to be in the middle of the night!

Andrew's flat was on the top floor of a seven-floor block. It was small but adequate and he was at pains to point out that through a corner of the living room window you could just see, over the neighbouring rooftops, a tiny patch of blue sea which Andrew assured him, was the Bosphorus. Occasionally, one could also see a ferry boat or a lesser beast of the water, moving in and out at great speed.

On the day after his arrival, Gordon was taken to see Ayios Sophia which had once been the glory and triumph of Christianity with its splendid dome making it one of the wonders of the ancient world. It was now unhappily reduced to being an unsatisfactory museum piece with various Muslin accretions.

After visiting it, they both walked across the fairly new Galata bridge which had replaced the former one with its shops and stalls but which had been destroyed by fire. As they were almost halfway across, and Andrew was pointing out landmarks on either side of the Golden Horn, Gordon suddenly realised that his only interest in life for the moment was to find, as quickly as possible, a public toilet. However, before he discovered one, near the far end of the bridge, the rear of his white shorts were stained brown and he realised to his dismay that this was the onset of a severe attack of diarrhoea. It was an embarrassing moment fearing that people walking behind him would notice. There was only one thing to do: return to the flat in some haste! Unfortunately it did not end there, for Gordon was unable to go out again for the next two days.

When finally he recovered, it was time to leave Istanbul and take the bus inland to Goreme in Cappadocia. This, said Andrew, was to be their main destination.

It was well on in the evening when they walked down to the main bus station where they found that they had to wait a while for their coach, the 8.30pm to Ankara and on to Cappadocia. The Istanbul bus station was a place of utter chaos. There were luxury coaches, dolmuses, battered old buses, small vans and lorries all waiting or slowly moving in or out amongst crowds of people standing around and bidding farewell to their relatives and friends. One group of young people were banging drums and singing and throwing one another up in the air. Permeating this scene of mayhem was the powerful stench of stale urine, supposedly due to people having been taken short on descending from their coach! Some of the enormous long distance coaches, the lions of the road, were manoeuvring between the smaller vehicles and groups of people.

After finally locating their coach, Gordon and Andrew settled down for the twelve hour journey. At frequent intervals the conductor of the coach would walk down and sprinkle everyone with lavender water and distribute cold plastic sachets of drinking water. Then every few hours there would be a fifteen minute stop at an all-night surprisingly sophisticated garage where there were shops, a restaurant, fruit stalls and toilets. At the first of these stops Gordon got out in order to go to the loo. He followed some of the male passengers to a door in the wall of a brick windowless cream painted building, next to the restaurant. However, as he approached he saw to his amazement that the men he was following had removed their shoes and before, in his sleepy state, he could back out, he found himself standing at the back of a small mosque which was nearly full of people – all men – on their knees in prayer.

Mosques are always well carpeted and if a good Muslim is unable to go to the mosque for the five calls for prayer each day, he can get out his prayer mat and kneel on that. This is the main reason why the carpet industry flourishes in Turkey and other Muslim countries. Bearing in mind the quite rigid discipline for the devout Muslim, the provision of a small mosque at the service stations was clearly serving a good and practical need.

The coach finally approached Goreme and by this time the sun was well up. Everyone in the coach began to move, to stretch themselves, yawning and slowly gathering together the various small items of luggage and personal possessions that had dropped to the floor or lay scattered on the few vacant seats.

Outside, as Andrew and Gordon looked through the now uncurtained coach window, the scene was almost Martian. The whole area seemed to be covered with a strange volcanic soil which at first sight seemed barren, but on looking closer was producing vegetation, and was in fact, one of the main agricultural regions of Turkey. Then, arising from it the solidified lava and volcanic earth had given rise to unusual undulating formations which were punctuated with clusters of pillars of rock protruding in steep conical, and almost comical, shapes. Many people in the past, and some even in the present, as Gordon and Andrew were to discover, had made their homes within these cones and Christians, in the early years of the church, had constructed churches out of them. Unfortunately, many of them through lack of use, had deteriorated into pigeon houses.

The journey by a local bus, a dolmus, from Neveshir to Goreme, brought them to the heart of Cappadocia. Here, some of the ancient rock-hewn dwellings had been modernised and were advertised as having accommodation with bed and breakfast and some even with full board. It seemed a strange blend of the primitive and modern: cave-dwellers and the twentieth century package tourist.

The fairy chimneys, as they were sometimes referred to, which had been created out of the soft lava rocks weathered by wind and rain, gave a weird and other wordly aspect to the whole region.

Andrew suggested walking a little away from where the bus had deposited them. Seated near them on the bus had been a lady of unknown nationality who seemed to be clad in what could best be described as kitchen foil. It was a silvery colour and seemed to be glued firmly to every contour of her somewhat copious body. Because of this she clearly had some difficulty getting out of the bus. Gordon remarked that she must have been sweating considerably beneath her tight wrapping.

They were just adjusting their rucksacks when the person in question turned to them and spoke in good English, "If you're looking for somewhere to stay I suggest you go up that road," and she pointed to a road at right angles to the one by which they had approached Goreme. "There are several good bed and breakfast and guest houses up there. It's all right, I've not got shares in them," she added, "but I've lived here for a while and I've got to know the good ones. Some of these Turks, you know, are out to make money – and I really don't blame them." With that comment she strode off in the opposite direction.

"What a strange person," remarked Gordon. "But I see no reason why we shouldn't take her advice."

Less than ten minutes walk away they saw on the left of the road up a steep incline, a cave dwelling and near it the sign "Traveller's Cave Pension".

"That would be ideal," said Andrew. "Let's see what the price is."

They approached the owner who lived in an adjoining cave dwelling, but before having an opportunity to discuss questions of finance, on discovering that they had just travelled overnight from Istanbul, he insisted on sitting them at a table in front of his dwelling and set before them coffee and a plate of bread, cheese, butter, a hard boiled egg and jam. By this time Gordon's appetite seemed to have returned to normal and they both showed their appreciation by consuming everything.

He was a friendly man by the name of Yuksel, in his early forties, a little on the skinny side for a Turk and with big watery eyes and a confident manner.

"Got any girls with you?" he asked.

"No, there are just the two of us," replied Andrew.

"Ah," and he looked curiously at them, "My main hobby, you know, is sex. I've had five girl friends: different nationalities, but the Japanese was the best because she was nice and quiet. You ought to have girl friends, you know. I could introduce you to one or two perhaps tomorrow."

"I think we're OK really," Andrew quickly interrupted. "You see, we're just interested in seeing the sights here in Goreme and round and about – thanks all the same."

By then Yuksel was leading the way to the cave-room they were to occupy. Before they arrived at it he told them that it had two beds, a toilet and a perpetually hot shower. This, he said, was unusual given the hot climate, and still more, thought Gordon, in such an unusual setting. It was facing the unmade-up road and set back some ten metres from it. It seemed to protrude from the surrounding rocks, but was unlike them in that it had a pointed roof above the front opening, the roof being also part of the solid rock face. Yuksel opened a door and inside they realised they were really in a cave.

They soon settled in, recovered from their journey and began to appreciate the advantages of such living. There were no creaking boards above, no sounds from an adjacent room and just one small window and door looking out onto a small terrace and a view of many more of the extraordinary freaks of nature where some of the early Christians lived and hid and spread the Gospel.

Yuksel told them that their "house" was well over a thousand years old and he pointed out some religious wall paintings in his own cave. Gordon noticed two curious holes in the wall either side of a small alcove in their own cave. They were at slightly different levels. Asked if they were for tying up animals, "No," laughed Yuksel. "That cave used to be my family's house and that was where my mother had a cradle and where I myself was rocked gently, suspended from those holes"

Yuksel then proceeded to tell them that his parents had been Egyptian and his father had come to Turkey mainly because he was an authority on the pyramids and wanted to find out more about the underground cities in Cappadocia. He had thought that there might have been a link between the two ancient civilisations. Andrew pricked up his ears at this as the pyramids also fascinated him. He was convinced that some of them, Cheops in particular, dated from much earlier than many people thought.

Yuksel continued, "There were," he said, "over two hundred of them although not all had been explored and some, it was thought, had been hewn out of the solid rock, not with metal tools but with stone and this would put them at several thousand years before Christ. Later they were used by the Hittites when they were attacked by the

Phrygians and then, much later again, by the Christians escaping from the Arabs.

Andrew was, by his 'umming' and 'aahing', greatly interested in all that Yuksel was recounting but Gordon decided to leave them to continue their conversation whilst he withdrew for a further spell in the horizontal.

He was resting on his bed in the cave, pondering on what he had heard and the fascinating experience of being in this ancient dwelling place, when he had a strange sensation. He was no longer in the ancient cave but as he looked up the roof seemed to slope up, far above him, to a point. He looked around and the walls were certainly slanting in from a distance away from him. It seemed as if he were on the ground at the base of a pyramid-shaped building. Strange effects were sometimes caused by pyramids. What effect would it have on him?

Startled, for a moment, he sat up. He remembered other things he had read about the pyramidal shape. What were they? He couldn't recall them at that moment. These thoughts and other vague recollections skimmed through his mind. Was he asleep? Was he dreaming? Was he transported to the pyramid of Cheops in Egypt? He lay quite still looking up at what seemed to be the point of the pyramid. Then he heard Andrew's voice. "Hi, Gordon! Have you had a good sleep?"

"Yes," he found himself replying, "but I've only been here a few moments!"

"Nearly three hours," replied Andrew.

"I can't believe it," said Gordon. "I've had another strange experience to do with this cave we're in. Had you noticed that it's been cut into the shape of a pyramid. Look up there."

"Yes," said Andrew, peering in the gloom of the cave up to the ceiling. "It certainly has been strangely cut with those four sloping sides."

Gordon continued, "I was thinking about the Great Pyramid in Egypt and the effects it has on people." He paused and then added, "You know, I feel fantastic now. All that feeling of sickness and nausea has gone. In fact, I feel as if I could climb a mountain or do anything. I'm sure it must be due to this shape above us. "

"Or it could be because you've had a good sleep which you needed, and topped up with a strong imagination," said Andrew. "I must admit," he added, "I'm just a little sceptical of these experiences of yours."

"Yes, but you saw the ghost at Fountains, didn't you? Do you remember - three years ago?"

"Well, yes, but that was different – oh, I don't know."

"And then," went on Gordon, "you must admit that there is a mystery about pyramids and especially the measurements of Cheops. What was it you once told me?"

"Yes, it's certainly true that our British system of measurement is to be found within the Great Pyramid. The basis of both is pi or 22 over 7. This applies also to the Golden Section found in nature and in many works of art."

The conversation was becoming involved, but Gordon wanted to hear more. He somehow felt that there must be a connection between the mystique of numbers and the strange experiences he'd been having. He still reflected occasionally on the curious happening at Dorchester with the Jesse window and the words of King David. Although three years had passed it still seemed very real to him.

"The Lord is compassion and love." If this was true of God, how did all these other mysterious facts fit in? The God of science and technology? The God who inspired people who were great artists and poets and writers? He thought then of the Irish tramp that he and Andrew had encountered on their cycling holiday in England. How did it all fit in? Or did it? He was beginning to think that perhaps there was no pattern, no unifying factor, no binding force behind all these different occurrences.

Andrew was continuing with his mathematical exposition on the pyramids. "The Great Pyramid of Cheops," he continued, "that pyramid has always fascinated me. Its proportions coincide exactly with the dimensions of the globe," he went on to say. "It was partly my interest in this that made me, initially, go in for engineering."

"Go on, explain what you mean," said Gordon, who was beginning to become interested. He hadn't heard Andrew speak about all this before.

"Well, to begin with," continued Andrew, "the Great Pyramid of Cheops almost certainly dates back, not just two or three thousand years BC, but more likely to the twelfth century BC. Erosion, which is evident, indicates 10,000 to 11,000 BC and this was when the earth was originally in perfect alignment with the Pyramid. You see, the sun's magnetic field reverses every 3,740 years and this causes the earth's crust to twist around on its axis. The next magnetic reversal is due to occur in 2012.

The Pyramid, and especially that with the proportions of Cheops, is not only of fundamental dimensions, but it produces most interesting effects." Andrew was warming to his subject. He continued, "It can produce within itself a resonance or frequency. For some reason or other, and we don't know how or why, there's a change in the molecular structure of objects placed inside it. Water, for example, tastes better. Razor blades become sharp again. Plants grow better. This applies to any pyramid, but particularly to one constructed according to the proportions of the Great Pyramid of Egypt. The force centre, if one can call it that, is very roughly one third up from the base, and my guess is that it corresponds to the proportion known as the Golden Section. This is known as "phi" after the Greek artist who used it a great deal in his sculptures. Pythagorus thought it was the basis of all proportions in the human body, as also did Leonardo da Vinci and many others. Michelangelo claimed that a piece of sculpture should be pyramidic.

Then, what is most interesting of all, is that in the Great Pyramid, Pi, 3.142 and Phi, 1.618, come together, both being important dimensions in its construction. However, as I've just said, any pyramidal shape can have interesting effects. Sleep under a pyramid and you sleep better. And, your psychic powers are stimulated. That ought to interest you, Gordon, with your mystical experiences; although I don't recall that you were sitting under a pyramid when we visited Dorchester Abbey."

"Oh, and I forgot to say," he continued – clearly this could almost be termed his pet subject, "Just near here, as Yuksel was telling us, when you fell asleep, in Capaddocia, was the ancient Hittite Kingdom and the Hittites excavated several thousand years BC those great underground cities, some of which you can still see today. These were, and still are on several levels, some as many as 19, with upper levels where people lived, lower levels for storage of food, and then there were carefully constructed air shafts, waste shafts, chimneys and wells, and even a hospital. There was even a telephone system which consisted of tiny holes pierced through the rock from level to level so that there could be communication especially when there was attack from above. But what is really interesting is that there was almost certainly a link between the Hittites and Egypt, as the bordering Canaan country was controlled by Egypt."

"Do you think, then," said Gordon, "that the pyramid shape comes into some of these strange constructions we see here around us?"

"It could be, it could be," said Andrew, "but it certainly has here in this particular cave."

At this point Yuksel appeared in the doorway. "I'm not cooking supper tonight," he announced, "but I invite you both to come with me to a very special restaurant where we can catch the fish. Are you good at fishing?"

Both gave a non-committal reply to this question, but accepted the invitation, although Gordon with some hesitation, as he felt he still wanted to treat his stomach with great respect.

When the time to eat came, they piled into Yuksel's small car and set off. To their amazement, they saw standing by the roadside just a short distance away the silver covered lady who had got off the bus with them.

"This is my friend, Yolanda," Yuksel introduced them. She smiled and got in the car. She no longer wore her silver covering, but was clad in a shoulderless yellow dress which only partly covered her breasts.

Yuksel turned round to Gordon and Andrew: "You should find girl friends, both of you" he said, "Or, perhaps, you're gay?" he added.

"Just good friends," said Gordon. "We've known each other since school days together."

"Hm – but it's good to have girlfriends, isn't it, sweetie?" he turned to Yolanda at his side and Gordon and Andrew could see from the back seat that he was clasping her hand and then stroking her thigh.

After a few moments they arrived at their destination. It was a restaurant surrounding a well-like structure about 12 foot square and waist high in the centre of a courtyard. Gordon peered over the edge and saw swimming around, a considerable number of quite fat fish. These, they were told, were imported from the Black Sea and kept alive in this confined space. One of the restaurant helpers had a net on a pole and two others were trying to sweep the fish into the net. Yuksel invited Gordon and Andrew to catch a few fish which they, unfortunately, had no luck in doing. Yuksel caught six and these were later cooked over a grill and eaten with potato salad and beans. It was an appetising meal.

Yolanda said little. Perhaps she was a little embarrassed at Yuksel's advances in front of two strangers.

"We don't often have English people in this place," remarked Yuksel, "although there was one man two years ago – he was Irish, but that's almost the same, isn't it? Yes, he was a great character. He stayed three nights in the cave where you are. He had a great voice: used to sing and wrote poetry. Then, one morning, I went to see him – in the cave where you are staying," he added again, "and found him dead in the bed. Had a heart attack. Had lots of complications reporting his death and getting him buried. Had to inform the British and then the Irish authorities. He had no relatives. Very strange. A wanderer. Hardly any luggage."

"What was his name?" asked Gordon.

"Some name I can't remember," said Yuksel. "Oh, yes, his first name was Francis. Man about sixty, with a great beard."

Andrew looked at Gordon. They were each having the same thought.

"When was this?" asked Gordon.

"About two years ago. Yes, it was a hot summer. Yes, two years ago," he repeated.

"I bet that was the man we met on our cycling tour three years ago," said Gordon.

"Where's his grave? Where is he buried?" asked Andrew.

"Here, just over there, behind those trees," replied Yuksel. "Finish your meal and I'll show you. "

It was quite dark by the time they had finished and Yuksel led them along a path to the nearby burial place and pointed to a small piece of wood set in the ground They could hardly see it, but on looking closer, they could just make out the name "Francis Buckhurst-Hill: died 29/06/2006."

"It's a strange coincidence that we should have met him on the road three years ago. That was not long before he came here and died."

Yuksel, who was standing by them with his arm around Yolanda's waist, said, "He left a small and dirty notebook which was found in his pocket. I gave his clothes away......."

"You threw them away," interrupted Yolanda. "They were so dirty."

"Yes, but I kept the notebook. It's somewhere at home. You can have it if you like. I don't really know why I kept it."

They returned back to their caves, Yuksel taking Yolanda into his own cave-dwelling, presumably for the night. However, before he bid them good night he brought a small soiled half-screwed up notebook which he handed to Gordon. "There it is. Take it. I don't want it."

After he had gone Andrew opened the little notebook which was mostly written in and comprised a series of poems and songs written out in neat script. It included the song with which the writer had regaled Andrew and Gordon on the road towards London. A few pages at the end of the notebook were blank except for the last page which was written in. It was not a poem, but headed, "My Will and Testament; Important Directions".

Andrew began to read it aloud to Gordon:

"I have nothing to leave to anyone but I hope to end my days on this earth at Eziat near the end of the Central Line out of London. Eziat gives the answer to my many questions. It is where I have been made welcome, and where I hope, eventually, to end my days, if God wills. Signed: Francis B-H."

"Sad that he didn't make it, isn't it?" said Gordon. I wonder what the place is that he writes about. I've never heard the name before."

"No, perhaps we could go and investigate next time we're in London." There was a pause as they both made ready for bed under the pyramid.

""Hope you sleep well," said Andrew. "The pyramid should help."

They little imagined the situation one of them would find himself in on a later occasion beneath a ceiling of pyramids.

It was the following morning that Gordon opened up the conversation with Andrew. "You know," he began, "I've been reflecting on those experiences I've had and that you know about, and in which you've been partly involved as well."

They were seated outside their cave-lodging downing coffee and, between gulps, drinking in the amazing vista of strange and remarkable shapes all around them. Gordon continued, "There was the experience in Dorchester with the Jesse window. But then, you know, long before that, when I was a child, I had the experience of flying. Whenever I mentioned this to anyone it has always been met with incredulity and put down to my imagination. But I know I had the experience of taking off at the top of a staircase and floating down. I remember once reading in a book by Elizabeth Goudge ["The Dean's Watch" p.26] that this was some echo of powers possessed in the innocent morning of the world when spirit and not body was the master."

Gordon glanced at Andrew, who seemed to be listening attentively, so he continued, "You know, I'm convinced that mankind originally had certain powers that became atrophied."

"And you think you may have some of those powers?" queried Andrew with a note of cynicism in his voice.

"Well," said Gordon, "I think everyone, whether they realise it or not, probably has something of them. You for example; I know you didn't have the experience that I had in Dorchester Abbey, but you did see and hear that ghost at Fountains in Yorkshire. And then there's the extraordinary coincidence of hearing about the death of that old tramp, or should I say, wanderer, here in this very place. You know, that's a very extraordinary coincidence. And then, what do you make of the peculiar effects of this pyramid shape we're sleeping under?"

"But that only affected you, Gordon," Andrew was quick to say.

Gordon appeared not to have heard, but continued: "You know when I was at school there was an RE teacher who used to talk about original sin. It didn't mean anything to me then, but now I begin to wonder if there's not something in it. Perhaps certain powers we now call clairvoyance, telepathy and all sorts of other signs and wonders, like seeing people who have died and those appearances Catholics talk about of the Virgin Mary appearing to certain people: all those may be quite genuine experiences for certain people, and," he added, "I know the experiences I've had are authentic."

At that point Yuksel appeared, apologising that it was already mid-morning and he had to go to the local market for food, no doubt accompanied by his lady friend.

Andrew and Gordon had already agreed that they would, later that day, have to catch the night bus back to Istanbul. Gordon would return to England whilst Andrew would resume his work in Turkey.

"I'm sorry to hear that," said Yuksel. "Perhaps you will come again – and if you ever find anyone who knew that Irishman who died here, you could give them the notebook. I'm glad you've taken it. It had been on my mind."

They said goodbye, with kisses on both cheeks, finished their coffees, packed their luggage and set off.

Several weeks later, having resumed his teaching and having a free day, Gordon decided that he would go to the mysterious sounding place mentioned in the old Irishman's message in his notebook: Eziat. He had written that it was beyond the end of the Central Line out of London. Furthermore other events in his life had conspired to make his return to England even more eventful.

Chapter 5 – Coincidence?

Edward and Betty Snaresbrook were seated in a small room facing a window which gave on to the dull cream plastered wall of the adjacent building. No direct sunlight could creep in to brighten the grey walls of the room, in no way enhanced by several nondescript and faded prints of sea-side scenes. The only bright and cheerful colours were provided by the untidy pile of glossy magazine left on a coffee table in the centre of the room.

Several people were already waiting when Edward and Betty arrived. They both sat down in silence. Edward looked pale and unwell, his complexion almost matching the grey of the walls, whilst Betty, his wife, was clearly anxious and kept screwing up her handkerchief, glancing towards her husband and saying, half to him and half to the wall opposite, "I wonder what he will say …. I wonder what he will say."

Edward responded with a grunt and murmured, "We'll see, my dear."

His wife was not calmed by this. She was a woman in late middle-age, her greying hair had once been well-attended by a good hairdresser, but at the moment it was drooping sadly over her forehead with few of its former curves and waves. "I was so worried," she went on "that we'd be late when that train was held up in the tunnel and we had to change to get here."

"Yes, but all was well," replied her husband. "We got here in time. Look we're having to wait."

At that moment a man came out form the inner door into the doctor's surgery and exclaimed to the world at large, "Well God help you lot!" and immediately added "Because this doctor won't!" as he strode out of the waiting room. At that moment the inner door opened again and a bright young receptionist announced, "Dr Farthing will see you now, Mr & Mrs Snaresbrook." Husband and wife got up and followed the girl into the doctor's inner sanctum.

"Sit down, and I do apologise for keeping you waiting, " he began. He was a man in his fifties, semi-bald and with large brown eyes which held his patients in a not-unkindly regard. He was one of the few doctors in that part of London who continued to practise on his own, as opposed to others who were part of a Group.

Someone had once remarked that he had an unusual name, to which he had replied, "It all depends on how you pronounce it!"

"Well now," he continued, addressing the Snaresbrooks, speaking slowly and carefully choosing his words. "I have received the results of the various tests you have had, Mr Snaresbrook, and I am afraid the outcome is not very good." He paused. Betty clutched tightly at Edward's hand. "You have a growth in the stomach and the liver is also affected. The condition of your stomach is such that an operation would really do no good and the liver, of course, is inoperable. This is bad news for you, and I am more than sorry to have to tell you."

Betty started dabbing at the tears that had sprung from her eyes. Edward stared thoughtfully in front of him. After a moment's silence, and still not looking at the doctor, he said, "That means it's terminal. So, how long have I got?"

"It's always difficult to say, but probably about six months," replied Doctor Farthing. "Of course," he continued, "there's all sorts of medication to alleviate pain and discomfort and, later on, I can put you in touch with the Macmillan nurses and any other form of care that you may need."

"Thank you, doctor," replied Edward. "As you must realise, I'm quite stunned and it'll take a little while for it to sink in."

"Yes," sobbed Betty, "we had so hoped that all would be well.....and we were thinking of going on a holiday in Italy next month, and, oh dear, I really don't know..."

"You should still be able to take your holiday," said Doctor Farthing. "In fact, that would be a very good thing to do. Just come and see me before you go."

"Thank you, doctor," said Edward. "Yes, thank you," added Betty. They both got up and left, the receptionist seeing them out.

"I really can't think straight. I'm numb," said Betty in a hushed voice as if she was in church.

Edward put his arm around her as they stepped out onto the pavement. What could he say?

Six months! Would it pass quickly ....and what then?

What must he do in the meantime? Edward was a practical sort of man. Already his thoughts were turning towards arrangements he should make to ease the strain on his wife, both during those few months he had left and afterwards.

Then the thought came to him – "What if the doctor was mistaken?" He had heard of such cases, and there were so many different sorts of cancer.

His reveries were interrupted by his wife saying, "Darling, the doctor did say we could still go on holiday. Let's build on that. Let's plan that when we get home."

So it was that, three weeks later Betty and Edward were at Heathrow. Edward was walking with a stick, but otherwise looked quite sprightly. Betty pulled their one suitcase on wheels as they made their way to the check-in.

They had decided to go to Rome. It had been largely Betty's idea. Her mother had been a Roman Catholic and Betty had been baptized in the church, had made her first Confession and Communion, but then the family had moved to a small village in Cornwall some distance from a Catholic church, and so the elements of faith had receded gradually from Betty's consciousness. In later years, if asked her religion, she would still say, though with some hesitation, "Er, yes, I suppose I'm Roman Catholic." But that was all it amounted to. That is until the drama of Edward's illness fell upon her. She asked herself, "Should she pray? Should she ask for a cure?" However, it seemed then almost like cupboard love with regard to God. But then, perhaps it would be as well to leave no stone unturned. She'd heard one of her friend's who was a Catholic, tell her to pray to Pope John Paul, the popular Pope who had died earlier that year. "Pray to him for a miracle for Edward," her friend had said. She had thought about it and decided that it would be appropriate to go to Rome where the Pope had lived and where he was buried, and pray to him there. After all, there was nothing lost in doing that – and, you never knew, a lot could be gained.

And, anyway,, Edward and she could enjoy a good holiday together in the city which was so full of interest. They might also be able to fit in a visit to Florence – she'd always wanted to go there. And then there was Pompeii and Assisi. She stopped herself. After all, it was to be mainly for Edward's benefit; what would he like to do?

They were finally on the plane. They had a window and middle seat, Betty taking the middle of the three, and just after settling in a man took up the aisle seat. Betty noticed immediately that he was wearing a clerical collar. He smiled and commented on the wet weather they had been experiencing. "I hope it'll be better than this in Rome," he said. "Is it your first visit?" he added.

Betty replied in the affirmative. He seemed a sympathetic type, although she found the black suit and the Roman collar a little awe-inspiring. They were soon at the end of the runway and the jet engines grew to a roar and the Boeing 737 started speeding down the runway.

Two elderly ladies were seated behind Betty and Edward, and Betty heard one of them say, "This is when I get quite nervous."

"Oh, it's all right dear," replied her companion, "We've got a priest sitting just in front of us!" At which the friendly priest in question, who had also overhead the conversation, half-turned and said "A fat lot of good I'd be if the plane crashed!"

He then smiled at Betty and added in a quieter voice, "Some people, you know, have a simple faith which borders on superstition." He then added, "Someone once said that there are no atheists on a plane that's about to crash."

"Yes," thought Betty, "that could very well be her attitude when thinking of God and a possible cure for Edward." However, she said nothing to the priest, who had proceeded to open up his prayer book and clearly wished not to be interrupted further.

The two hour flight was soon over, and after polite goodbyes to their travelling companion, Edward and Betty found their way to their hotel which was in a narrow side road just off the Piazza Navone. However the journey there had not been without an initial trauma.

The airport bus had deposited them near the forecourt of Rome's busy main line railway station. From there they had followed directions and taken the No 64 bus which went in the direction of St. Peter's.

Standing close to Edward, Betty noticed a man who had puzzled her by having a towel over one arm. Only later when they got off the bus near their destination did Edward find that his camera case slung over his shoulder was unzipped and the camera was missing. It was an unfortunate welcome to Rome, but the hotel receptionist belatedly warned them that the Number 64 was a notorious playground for pick-pockets and thieves.

The journey and the incident on the bus had taken its toll on Edward, so, on finding their modest hotel room in the via Loutari, he flopped onto the bed and was soon asleep. Meanwhile Betty, who felt full of energy and wanting to explore as soon as possible, having unpacked their suitcases, decided to venture out. She would have preferred to be with Edward, but already she knew that one day in the near future she would have to be on her own. This holiday in Rome was to be the last with him, but it would, for her, be a kind of transition to when she would be alone, without him. But no, she must not think of that. It seemed almost an act of disloyalty on her part to countenance such thoughts even for a moment.

Meanwhile, she would enjoy her walk, come back refreshed and they could go together to a pleasant restaurant in the Piazza Navone, indulge in a good Italian meal and a bottle of Valpolicella.

It must have been over an hour and a half when Betty finally found her way back to the hotel. The time had passed quickly. She had walked for probably a mile or two, gazing into shop windows – mostly those selling clothes or food. She had ventured through the foreboding archway leading into the Pantheon. The Roman emperor, Hadrian, who was responsible for the wall between England and Scotland had rebuilt this in circular form. It had previously been a first century BC rectangular temple building. Apart from a few minor alterations Betty was seeing it in its original form. She found it gloomy and felt that Edward would have appreciated it more.

Edward had been an engineer before he took early retirement and he had wanted to see the Pantheon as there was a mystery about how its enormous dome, the largest until recent times, had been constructed. Perhaps, thought Betty, they could return there later. She little knew that this would be impossible.

The Piazza Navone she found far more interesting with its array of artists, casual entertainers, the great Bernini fountain with figures representing the four continents of Europe, Africa, Asia and American and the rivers, the Nile, Danube, Ganges and Plate, and all bordered by an enticing array of restaurants set out ready for the evening customers. Betty decided then to return to the hotel, and no doubt Edward, having rested would be ready to go out for dinner. They had saved money by not getting a taxi to their hotel, so perhaps they could indulge in a really good meal.

She found her way back to the hotel, got in the lift, went to their room, but as she opened their door she cried out in alarm for what first met her eyes was Edward spread out on the floor by the bed. She rushed to him. Was he breathing? Yes, he seemed to be. She called his name: "Edward, what is it? What's the matter?" His eyes remained closed and no sound came from him.

What should she do? She panicked. There was a telephone by the bed. She took it up, remembering that the receptionist spoke a little English.

"Please get me an ambulance – quickly" she almost shouted into the phone. "My husband is ill – very ill." At first the man at the other end did not understand. She repeated her demand, and finally made him realise what the problem was.

Some fifteen minutes later the ambulance men arrived, and having very briefly examined Edward, they got him onto a stretcher and he was being transported, with siren blaring, through the Roman rush hour traffic.

Betty stayed with him in the ambulance, trying to convey to the assistant, sitting in the back, what Edward was suffering from, although she was puzzled that the cancer could have brought on the collapse. After all, his doctor at home had assured her that all would be well if they went on holiday. Perhaps it was the strain of the journey. He did say he was tired.

Where were they going? She tried to ask the man next to her. She managed, after several attempts, to gather that they were bound for a hospital not too far away, the Gemelli. That was where the Pope was taken when he was shot in St Peter's Square. She remembered hearing about that. She was relieved: it sounded a good hospital.

Edward was still unconscious when they arrived there. Italian nurses and a doctor immediately surrounded him and Betty was shown into a side room. After what seemed to her an age, a doctor came in, and in halting English said to her, "Heart. Heart attack. Soon better. Two days. Perhaps three."

"Could I see him?" Betty asked.

"Later, later," replied the doctor.

"Later" turned out to be another two hours, but then when she was finally allowed into the room where they had moved him, she breathed a sigh of relief. He was conscious and able to speak.

"What happened dear? Where am I? I'm confused with all these "Ities" whom I can't understand."

Betty stayed with him a while before, exhausted herself, she returned to the hotel. The two days extended to four. Betty spent much of this time at the Gemelli, although Edward seemed disinclined or unable to talk very much. Between visits she decided to distract herself by exploring something of the eternal city. Saint Peter's and the Vatican were a must.

It was a Wednesday morning. She had phoned the hospital and promised to visit Edward in the afternoon. St Peter's was under a half-hour walk from the hotel, and as she arrived in the piazza in front of the basilica she saw that hundreds of chairs were set out ready for the weekly public audience with the Pope.

"How wonderful," she thought. "I'll stay here at least until he arrives." This turned out to be longer than she had anticipated. Meanwhile, long lists of various groups assembled there were read out, and each group of people mentioned would cheer and wave their flags or banners from some corner of the vast crowd that had by then assembled.

Finally, after nearly an hour and a half of expectant waiting, the white-cassocked, white-haired, shy and kindly figure of Pope Benedict appeared, standing in an open vehicle, moving slowly through the barricaded lines dividing up the crowd. After traversing every section of the crowded piazza, the Pope mounted the rostrum set in front of the main doors of St Peter's, and when the cheers had subsided, Betty thought he was going to speak. But no, the list of the pilgrims continued unabated for a further twenty minutes. This, Betty thought, was unnecessary and could have been reduced to the mention merely of the various countries, as opposed to six or seven people from the parish of the Sacred Heart in Malawi, or some such place.

Eventually, there was a pause and the Pope, after patiently waiting, read a passage from the New Testament on which he then commented. All this had then to be translated into six different languages before he finally gave his blessing, got into the popemobile and disappeared from view.

Well, she had been to an audience with the Pope and received his blessing, albeit together with several thousand others. That was something to tell Edward about. She decided to have a look inside St Peter's and in a rash moment, to go to the top of the dome. She liked high points and she'd be able to see all over Rome from there.

A lift took her part of the way up, and, to her amazement, she found, on the lower roof, a small souvenir shop and café. This could not be passed by without a visit. Further up was an arduous climb and she noticed that as the dome curved so did the mounting corridor, and so did the pilgrim, having almost to lean sideways to mount higher.

The view from the top was stunning, with the details of the Vatican gardens, many of the Roman landmarks, and almost swathed in the misty heat to the south, was the basilica of St Paul outside the walls. Edward had spoken to her about this, as he'd been told that it was the most interesting of all the churches. Perhaps she would go there the following day.

She was able to identify many other landmarks: both ancient buildings, mostly churches, as well as even more ancient ruins, such as the Forum and the Colosseum. She was reminded of the saying she had once heard, "If you're in Rome up to three years you're regarded as a monument, but longer than that you're looked upon as a ruin." Meanwhile, time was moving on and she must have a sandwich somewhere and get to the hospital. When she eventually arrived there, she found Edward asleep. She decided to wake him and tell him about the morning. He was interested and seemed pleased that she was seeing something of Rome.

"I'm not too bad," he said, "so you make good use of your time sight-seeing in the morning and you can come to seem me after lunch."

The next day Betty decided to explore the Roman transport system, so she took a bus and then the underground train to St Paul's outside the walls. It was all quite straightforward and she soon found herself standing before the impressive stone pile of the abbey adjoining St Paul's. This great church, in spite of a near-disastrous fire in the early nineteenth century, had retained its original columned nave and simple style all unhindered by later Baroque accretions. How Edward would have enjoyed this visit.

St Paul's tomb was under the high altar, but the apostle was martyred, beheaded, just over a mile from the basilica at a place called TreFontane. Betty decided to take the underground train again and go there. She found the Rome underground far superior, cleaner and pleasanter than the familiar Central line near their home in London.

At TreFontane she found the most magnificent Romanesque abbey church in Rome. Nearby stood a small Baroque church which marked the actual place where St Paul was martyred, and a small stone pillar on which it is reputed his head was cut off. This was probably not authentic, but at least the place where it occurred was beyond dispute.

After pausing in veneration before this, she went, partly out of curiosity to another building very near the church. It turned out to be the home of the Little Sisters of Charles de Foucauld. This didn't mean much to Betty, but seated just inside the open doorway was one of the Sisters dressed in a faded blue habit. She was writing, but looked up as Betty hesitantly entered.

"Bonjour, Madame," she greeted Betty.

"I don't speak French, Sister," responded Betty. "Only English".

The nun, who was probably in her mid-thirties, continued in somewhat stumbling English. "You are most welcome. This is the house where Charles de Foucauld, a French priest who became a hermit in the Sahara, stayed for a while." She went on to explain that it was now the headquarters of the Little Sisters of Jesus, one of several religious orders stemming from the spirituality of de Foucauld.

Brother Charles, she went on to tell Betty, came of a wealthy French family, lost his faith, but finally came back, when at the age of 28 years, he had a powerful conversion experience. He became a man of prayer which was centred especially on the Eucharist. This caused him to want to live like Jesus at Nazareth. Eventually, he did this by going to live in Algeria amongst the Tuareg people. Someone who knew him had quoted him as saying:

"I am not here in order to convert the Tuareg people at once but to try to understand them…..I am sure that the Good Lord will welcome into heaven all those who have been good and honest without them having to be Roman Catholic. You are Protestant, the Tuareg has no religious faith at all, the Tuareg are Muslim. I am convinced that God will welcome all of us if we deserve it."

The Sister could clearly have gone on enthusing about Charles de Foucauld and his life, but Betty felt she should get back to the hospital. She thanked the Sister for her welcome and took the small prayer card that had been offered her. "I will pray for your husband," said Sister, "Au revoir."

She returned to the hospital and, after discussion with the doctor, it was decided that Edward was well enough to risk flying back to England. However, it had been made clear to Betty that he should immediately be admitted to hospital, or even a hospice, in England, as the cancer seemed to have accelerated and he would need especial care and fairly constant nursing.

The two hour flight was nightmarish, and was not helped when the plane encountered bad weather over the Alps. At one point, the cabin crew were told to be seated and fasten their seat belts just before the plane seemed suddenly to drop over a hundred and fifty feet. A middle-aged American business man seated next to Betty exclaimed, "My, I've been travelling most of my life, but I've never before experienced anything like that."

Edward seemed to be in a semi-soporific state for most of the journey, and one of the airport's motorised buggies for invalids was awaiting his arrival at Heathrow. Betty, with the help of the hospital, had made arrangements beforehand for him to be admitted to St Marys hospital in Paddington.

Soon after his arrival, Betty was seated by his bed holding his hand, but refraining from saying very much. Edward was by this time wired up with tubes visible all around him.

"How was it going to end?" wondered Betty. The cancer seemed to have attained an advanced state. Yes, she knew he was terminally ill, but the waiting, the wondering, was painful for her as well as for him. "What was he thinking now?" Edward had never been a very communicative man. She had nearly always had to take the initiative in conversation.

Then she began reflecting on their decision to go to Rome, and how disastrous it had turned out. She had certainly seen some of the sights she had always heard about and wanted to visit, but always she had had the feeling of emptiness and restraint and aloneness because she had been on her own.

At that moment a black suited clergyman came over to them. He smiled and introduced himself: "I'm Colin Shepherd , the local C.of E. priest. I gather your husband – he is your husband, I presume – has only recently been admitted, and I thought I'd drop in to say 'hello'. I'm actually just standing in for the regular chaplain."

"My husband's not really well enough to talk," responded Betty, "but I'm pleased to see you." She looked at Edward who still had his eyes closed, and then, to her alarm, the colour of his cheeks seemed to turn blue and his whole body, for a moment, shook. A that point one of the nurses looked in.

"Father", she shouted at the priest, "You're standing on the oxygen tube!" and as she yelled out, she as quickly pushed the bewildered clergyman out of the way. He apologised, and clearly thought he'd do better to withdraw completely. The nurse also apologised, although she had, in fact, saved the day. Adequate oxygen was restored and Edward opened his eyes and to Betty's amazement began to speak.

"Sorry, my dear, to give you all this trouble and worry," he said. "You know I was vaguely conscious of what was going on. I wondered what that clergyman wanted. I suppose he thought I was dying." He paused. "Well, perhaps I am......What's going to happen then?" he added.

Betty, with her Roman Catholic upbringing, replied without hesitation, "Darling, you'll go to heaven and be with all the saints."

"I find that difficult to believe," said Edward slowly. His eyes closed again. Betty said nothing. "If only he had faith," she thought. "He'd be able to face death calmly." But then, she added to herself, he did seem to be pretty calm, although you could never really tell what he was thinking.

She remembered a programme she'd seen several years ago when Gwen Frangcon-Davies, a former well known actress, was, at the age of 97, being interviewed and she was asked, "Well, Miss Davies, you are at a certain age when death cannot be too far off. Are you afraid of dying?" The elderly actress had hesitated, smiled and replied "Well," she said, "I supposed you're always a little nervous of doing something for the first time."

Betty had found this very consoling. She must recount it to Edward and see how he reacted.

She staying on by his bedside another half an hour, but his short period of being 'with it' did not return. The doctor came and spoke with her, advising her to go home and have some rest. He could give her no sure idea what the outcome might be: heart or cancer, which of the two would defeat him first.

It was a week later when Betty was on the Central Line and had just got out at Notting Hill Gate, mounted the escalator in order to change onto the District Line heading for Paddington and the hospital when her mobile phone started singing out. She thrust her hand in her bag, pulled out the phone, and stopped just at the top of the escalator.

It was the ward sister. "Yes, what is it?" she asked, immediately imagining the worst. "Your husband, Edward, has taken a sudden turn for the worse," the Sister's voice came over the phone.

"I'll be there within a quarter of an hour; I'm already on my way," Betty managed to shout down the phone.

"Oh God," she thought. "It doesn't sound very good." She should have asked for more details, but she had swiftly switched off the phone and was rushing over to the District Line train. It seemed to be an age arriving, and it was a good twenty minutes before she finally entered the ward and was greeted by the sister.

"Mrs Snaresbrook," she said, "I think you should be prepared for the worst. I don't think your husband is going to pull through this time."

"Is he conscious?" demanded Betty.

"No, and he's in no pain. You'll see." She led Betty into the side ward and she could see immediately what the sister had meant. A doctor was standing by the bed. He turned as soon as Betty came in. "Mrs Snaresbrook," he said, "I think your husband has only a very short while to live. There is nothing more we can do for him. I'm sorry." At that he left the room and Betty was alone with her husband. She took his hand. She began to pray, at first silently, and then aloud. She remembered that she had been told once that when someone is apparently unconscious, they can, nevertheless, often hear you. She prayed the Our Father, she prayed to Our Lady –"pray for us now and at the hour of our death", - she prayed to St Jude, the patron of hopeless cases. She remember the prayer card that the Sister had given her in Rome and which she still carried in her handbag. It was a prayer by the French priest, Charles de Foucauld, whom the Sister in Rome had told her about, but it had been translated into English. After a moment's searching, her handbag not being the tidiest, she found it and started reading it aloud –

"Father, I abandon myself into your hands;
do with me what you will.
Whatever you may do, I thank you:
I am ready for all, I accept all.
Let only your will be done in me,
And in all your creatures.
I wish no more than this, O Lord.
Into your hands I comment my soul;
I offer it to you with all the love of my heart,
For I love you, Lord, and so need to give myself,
To surrender myself into your hands,
Without reserve and with boundless confidence,
For you are my Father."

At the last few phrases her voice trembled and almost faded. Edward had opened his eyes very slightly, a faint smile around his lips, and with a feeble gasp his eyes closed again and she realised that his breathing had ceased.

She continued to sit staring at him, the prayer card still in her hand, and the tears began flowing in great drops down her cheek. How long she sat like that she had no idea, but it was probably only a few minutes before the nurse returned and quickly disappeared to report the situation to higher authority.

For the next few days Betty was kept busy with arrangements for the funeral. Both she and Edward had very few relatives. Her closest was a brother, Stephen Newby, who lived with his family in Australia, but Edward had no relatives, and they had had no children, having married when both were in their forties. She phoned her brother, Stephen, but whilst he was very sympathetic, she didn't think it sounded as if he would make the long journey to England for the funeral. One of Edward's friends from the firm where he used to work helped her with the paperwork necessary on the occasion of a death. Edward had wanted to be cremated, so this was arranged for just six days later.

Meanwhile Betty, whilst being busy with a multitude of things to do, as well as receiving innumerable callers, friends and neighbours, in the evenings she had time, when all was quiet, to reflect on the events of recent weeks.

Had it been a terrible mistake going to Italy for that holiday? The two journeys there and back had certainly taken their toll on Edward. If only they had gone nearer to home, somewhere in England. And when they were in Rome and Edward was in the hospital, she had spent time exploring and visiting the Roman sites when perhaps she should have spent longer with Edward. If only.....her thoughts were crowded with 'if onlys'.

But no, she should make an effort to think positively. After all there was that wonderful moment when Edward had looked at her as she read the prayer just a few seconds before he died. And the nun in Rome who had given her the prayer. They were certainly 'positives', and moments to remember. She felt that God had been present then.

Perhaps it had all worked out in His way.....but she could never be sure.

Her faith, though weak, as a Catholic, gave her some reassurance. It then came to her that she should go to church, go to Mass and pray for Edward. After all, he was not going to have a Requiem Mass. He hadn't wanted that: just a simple service at the crematorium.

It was Tuesday, just two days before the funeral. She would go to Mass today, and maybe speak with the priest. The crematorium had been booked by the funeral directors, but she had still to decide on who was to conduct the service. Edward, she felt, whilst he was against a church service, and certainly not a Catholic Mass, would not object to a Catholic priest leading a few prayers in the crematorium chapel – especially after what had happened just before he died. Betty kept pondering on the extraordinary incident of the prayer card she had been given in Rome and read out while Edward breathed his last breath.

She visited the hospital once more, to collect a few of Edward's belongings, to thank the staff, and she then called in at the nearby Catholic church. There was a lunchtime Mass in progress and when it was over she went into the sacristy to speak with the priest. It turned out to be a Father O'Leary, an Irishman who proved to be helpful and understanding when she explained the situation to him.

"Yes, no problem," he replied. "Do you want any hymns?" "They'll be Catholic prayers, of course," he added.

"No hymns, just a very simple service."

"O.K.," he said, "Give me your address, and I'll call in this evening to discuss a few details: about your husband, and what you'd like me to say."

"That would be fine", said Betty, "and thank you very much."

Father O'Leary kept his word, and all was arranged.

An unexpected number of people gathered in the chapel at Mortlake for Edward's cremation: people with whom he had worked, friends from Ealing where they lived, members of the golf club to which he had belonged, and a few people from Father O'Leary's church congregation. She invited them all to a nearby pub where she had ordered drinks and snacks. Edward would have approved of that.

★ ★ ★

It was nearly two years later and Betty was still finding it difficult to settle down to any sort of regular orderly life. All the correspondence and paper-work invariably necessary after a death had long since been done. She had no real hobbies. Her life had been so bound up with her husband. Friends would call, but it was difficult going out to socialise, as most social events involved couples. She felt lonely, isolated and bewildered. She missed Edward so much. She still regretted those days in Rome when she had not been with him and instead had been sight-seeing. The evenings were darkening and she dreaded their length when she would have no one with whom to talk. Television did not interest her: there was little worth viewing, and while she enjoyed reading, she soon became tired and sleepy and unable to concentrate no matter how interesting the book might be.

She resonated with the feelings of Dame Judi Dench, the actress whose husband had died. Dame Judi had once said, "I really need people around me all the time. As one gets older, it gets harder to be alone." Then one evening, in a rare moment of desperation, she had switched on the television and found herself viewing a nature programme about wildlife in Australia. She thought of her brother who lived in Brisbane. He was her only relative but they had not seen each other for nearly twenty years when he had emigrated. However, they had always kept in touch, although he had been unable to make the journey for Edward's funeral.

Yes, she would phone him and see if it would be possible to visit. He was married with two teenage youngsters. Perhaps there would not be room in the house. Anyway, she could but ask.

"Hello, is that you, Stephen?" she almost shouted down the phone.

"Yes," replied a sleepy voice "Who's that?"

"It's Betty, your sister from England."

"Oh, - well did you not know that it's only 4 o'clock in the morning here?"

"Oh, Stephen, I'm, so sorry," replied Betty, still shouting at the phone in spite of the clarity of the line.

She had not started off very well. She should have realised the ten hour time difference. Fortunately, Stephen was not too put out, and greeted her proposal of a visit quite positively. Yes, she would be welcome anytime, and they had a small spare bedroom which she could occupy. The house, he said, was not all that quiet. How could it be with teenage youngsters? She thought she would risk that and so, without further delay, she arranged her flight and in less than two weeks found herself airborne and bound for Brisbane.

She arrived at 9.30pm in the evening and anxiously looked at the waiting crowd of anonymous faces as she came through the arrivals barrier. Stephen had said he would meet her. Ah yes, there he was and with Sarah, his wife, and two young lads who were grinning and nudging each other as she approached and received the warm embrace of her brother and sister-in-law.

"Great to see you," said Stephen. "Had a good journey? Oh, and these are Gerry and John, whom you've never met, but I sent you photos."

"Hello Gerry. Hello John." Betty greeted her two nephews.

Gerry was sixteen and John fourteen. Both had long hair and smiled shyly at her.

"Hi," they both said. "Can we call you Betty?" added Gerry.

"Of course" she replied.

They made their way to the car park and Sarah insisted on Betty sitting in the front. Sarah was much younger than Stephen, who was only two years Betty's junior. He was 62. Like his sister Betty, he had married late, but he had waited until he had found and fallen in love with a real beauty. When they were married Sarah was only nineteen. In fact, she had been a pupil in the school where he taught, and while he had in no way disgraced himself, there had been comments and false judgements thrown around at the time. Sarah had left school and gone to London for over a year before returning to Brisbane and soon afterwards marrying Stephen.

Betty and her parents had not gone to the wedding with the excuse that Brisbane was too far to go, but the newly-wed couple had honeymooned in Europe, ending up in London where they had met Stephen's parents as well as Betty. The meeting with his parents had been brief and both parents had died soon after. Betty and Sarah had seen more of each other, and when Betty had become accustomed to the age difference, she began to realise what had attracted her brother, for Sarah was not merely attractive, but she had a considerable depth of character, could converse sensibly on most subjects, was an excellent tennis player and had learned how to be a good cook. These last two attributes had also without a doubt attracted Stephen.

The half-hour journey from the airport was taken up with the customary questions and answers about the journey punctuated with the boys shouting out various places they were passing which they thought would be of interest to Betty.

"There's the stadium…"

"…and there's the school I used to go to;"

"That's where Mom plays tennis."

"That's Sizzlers…"

"That's my favourite restaurant," added John.

It all seemed bewildering to Betty, tired as she was after the twenty-four hour flight. She felt she could not absorb any more.

When they finally arrived at their destination, she wanted, more than all else, to be quiet and to sleep. Sarah and Stephen's house was not a house as one would understand it in England. It was a spacious bungalow; but the word bungalow does not exist in Australia. A bungalow is a house, and this particular one was an ancient Queenslander house built on stumps with formerly an open but now covered verandah going around three sides of it. It was in a suburb known as Toowong, which Betty was told was an Aborigine word for a particular type of cuckoo, really a goatsucker bird which made a sound like "too-wong!"

As she climbed the few steps to go in, she began, in spite of her tiredness, to be sure that she had done the right thing in coming so far. And then an unexpected wave of lachrymose feeling nearly overcame her. Edward. How he would have enjoyed being there. He would have loved the warm climate, meeting the youngsters, his nephews by marriage, the whole atmosphere of the place and the welcome she was being given by Stephen and Sarah. Her sudden sadness almost brought tears to her eyes. That wouldn't do just as she was being shown her room and told that in just a few minutes, when she was ready, they would sit down to eat.

The meal was more than she wanted, having had quite a lot to eat whilst on the plane. Then, hardly ten minutes after having started, there was a ring at the bell and in walked a well-built grey-haired man wearing a wide-brimmed Australian bushland hat, which he removed as he greeted everyone.

"Hi, you folks! Hope I'm not intruding, but you told me one of your Pommy relatives was coming, and so I thought I'd just drop in to say 'hello'."

"Yes," said Stephen, "This is Betty, my sister – just arrived. Sit down and have something to eat."

"Thanks. That's great, but say, Steve, you didn't introduce me!"

"Sorry. Betty, this is Alfred, but he prefers to be called Alf. He's recently widowed and lives just a few doors away."

"Yes," added Alf, "and I often drop in. They're a great family. Been very good to me, especially when my wife got ill and died."

"My sister's been in a similar situation," said Stephen "and that's why she's over here, to take her mind off it for a bit."

"That's not really possible," countered Alf. "I know only too well."

At this point Sarah clearly thought it advisable to change to another topic. "Alf, did you watch the cricket this evening? We missed some of it but I gather England weren't in such good form." The conversation then moved along sporting lines with the two boys joining in. Sarah and Betty said little. Alf launched into a monologue of details of cricket matches played over the last twenty years. His memory for detail was phenomenal.

Betty felt her eyelids drooping. If Edward had been there he would undoubtedly have shown more interest in the cricket talk. But he wasn't.

"I'm sure you must be wanting to sleep." The meal was over and Sarah realised Betty's need for bed, and armed her up from the table. "Alf would go on all night if he could," she added. However, Betty noticed that, as she left the room, he had paused in mid-flow, and looked smilingly at her.

"See you again, soon," he called, "Have a good sleep!"

The next day, after a long and extended night, Betty surfaced and found her way to the terrace where a table was set for one. Sarah appeared and apologised that everyone had eaten earlier. Stephen had gone to his office in the city, the two boys were at school and Betty was pleased to find that she would be able to chat and get to know Sarah better.

Coffee and cereals and toast were brought out. It was just like back home in England. Sarah sat down with Betty and began asking about London today. When she had visited after she and Stephen were married, there had been such little time to see and appreciate many of the sights and she had been too preoccupied with her boyfriend to explore. They were well launched in conversation when the gate opened and to Betty's surprise, and slight disappointment, she recognised Alf of the previous night. His alcubra bush hat was set at a slightly rakish angle towards the back of his head and it was impossible to discern the expression on his face as he was wearing very dark and large sunglasses.

"Hi Sarah. Hi Betty. Great to see you again. Had a good sleep?" "

"Yes thanks: it's only fault was its brevity as my dear husband used to say".

And with that Alf seated himself at the table next to Betty. The three of them chatted amicably for a while until Sarah excused herself in order to arrange some food in the kitchen. As soon as she had gone Alf turned to Betty: "I was just wondering," he began, "if you'd like to have a look around the city. I hear it's your first stay out here. I could take you around and show you a few of the sights; although we've nothing historical like you have back home."

Betty was not sure how to respond to this. Perhaps Sarah had other plans. The latter returned at that moment and said that she purposely hadn't thought of anything in particular for the first few days, as she knew it took a while to recover from jet-lag and become accustomed to the change of climate.

"Perhaps tomorrow," replied Betty turning to Alf, "that is provided the family haven't arranged anything." "

No, today's Wednesday," replied Sarah, "We planned to take you out at the weekend – the rain forest and various other places. No, you go with Alf, if you feel like it."

Betty felt she could hardly refuse outright, so arrangements were agreed on for the following day. She had really wanted to have time to get to know the family, her relatives, better, but she supposed there would be plenty of opportunities for this during her stay.

Alf called for her the next day as arranged. She was still feeling the effects of the long flight, sleepy and disorientated. However, as she sat in Alf's car and he chatted on, telling her something about the places they were passing, she began to feel more relaxed. Driving on the left, noticing the shops and supermarkets and speaking English all contributed to her feeling almost at home.

Australia, she gathered, was a generous and easy-going country in which the traditions of both England and America blended together.

Brisbane itself was a busy skyscraper topped city, the centre of which was the Mall, a pedestrianised partly covered throughway. There were street entertainers and Betty was particularly interested in listening to an Aborigine playing his didgeridoo. There were not many Aborigines in Brisbane itself, Alf told her. They were mostly in settlements out in the bush. In all, in Australia, they were now only about one per cent of the total population, being well outnumbered by the invading British, as well as other nationalities. She noticed that there were vast numbers of Indonesian, Malaysian and Philippinos, as well as Japanese, who seemed to be mostly tourists. At an appropriate moment, Alf suggested that they should have a meal together. It was lunchtime and they went to Sizzlers. This turned out to be a restaurant where the main course could be ordered from a wide selection of meats and fish, and then having found a table, one served oneself to a starter, vegetables and salads to go with the main course, a selection of cheeses, desserts and, of course, drinks. Alf insisted on paying, but Betty noticed that it all turned out to be about one-third of the cost of a similar meal in London.

They were seated in a corner table. Alf had removed his hat and his dark glasses. "Now we can talk," he said.

Betty wondered what would come next.

"We're each in a very similar situation", he began, "and I really feel privileged and that it's God's will that we've met like this."

Betty wondered at that point if the whole encounter had been engineered by her brother and sister-in-law. Alf continued, "My wife died eleven months ago, and Steve was telling me that your husband died a while back. I was very happily married, as I guess you were too, so I just know how you're feeling at the moment."

Betty didn't really wish to share her feelings with someone who was, after all, almost a stranger. She let him talk, and this he found no difficulty in doing.

He had worked at the Jondaryan Woolshed which was in the Darling Downs, about one hour's journey inland from Brisbane. The Woolshed, he explained, was a huge sheep shearing centre built in 1861, but some twenty five years ago it had been converted into a historical museum and park. For some years Alf had acted as a guide to the many visitors who flocked there throughout the year. He used to show people the machinery and equipment that was once used, he would show them the original old schoolroom with its notices and rules and, as a grand finale, he would demonstrate the art of sheep-shearing with real live sheep.

One day, he went on to recount to Betty, his wife had driven out from Brisbane with him and they were returning on the motorway just twenty kilometres from the city when the front tyre of their car burst. They had been travelling at 100kms an hour. He was driving, and instinctively braked. However, this was not the best thing to have done. The car had swerved badly, careered off the road, turned over twice and ended up on a low embankment at the side of the road. His wife, in the passenger seat, was unconscious, and on arrival at the hospital pronounced dead. He, amazingly, had suffered only a broken arm and severe shock.

His family, two girls who lived in London, and a boy the youngest, who had just finished at university in Brisbane, were all utterly shattered. The girls had flown over for their mother's funeral, but had not stayed home as Elaine had a responsible job in the city and Shirley, the younger of the two, wanted to travel back with her sister. Shirley had not settled and was intent on seeing something of Europe before establishing herself in a permanent job. She had qualified at the L.S.E and didn't really know whether or not she wanted to remain in England, or what she wanted to do. So it was that Alf had been left to recover from the double shock of the accident and losing his wife, as well as partly blaming himself for the severity of the crash.

All this he poured out to Betty, and she had the impression that he had recounted this undoubtedly tragic story to many others over the past few months. Into his steady flow of words she had uttered suitably sympathetic "Erms" and "ohs" and "oh dears".

Alf was clearly a lonely man. This was understandable, although Betty remembered reading, only a few days before, that in the generous and easy-going country of Australia loneliness was becoming a problem.

This was surprising in such a hospitable and open society. She wondered if it was due to the increased materialism, self-concern and the undermining of the whole concept of neighbourhood and community.

After further accounts of his past life, Alf finally drove Betty back to Toowong, where she was glad to relax once again on her bed before enjoying a pleasant evening with the family.

She became a little concerned when on the following day Alf again turned up, wanting this time to take her on the City Cat, one of the river buses which plied frequently up and down the river passing through the city centre and stopping at convenient places en route. Betty found it difficult to refuse his invitation, although at the end of the day she had to admit that it had been interesting. At one point they had spent over an hour visiting the oldest building in Queensland, the Commissariat, which had been built in 1859 by some of the convicts over from England. She was interested, although horrified, to see evidence of the way they had been treated, often with heavy iron shackles around their ankles and in a confined space, those having committed the crime of stealing a neighbour's chicken had been shipped over from England and imprisoned, serving the same sentence as another found guilty of murder. Betty had been wanting to ask Alf if he was descended from one of the convicts, but decided that it would be better to remain in ignorance and merely guess at the truth.

The day was Friday, and she was relieved to know that Stephen and the family were arranging the following day to take her inland to the bush and the rain forest. They would take food with them, walk and put up for the night in a hotel. "You're not inviting Alf to come with us, are you?" Betty, somewhat fearfully, asked Sarah that evening. "Oh, no," she replied, "Anyway there wouldn't be room in the Toyota. Did you not get on too well with him?" she added.

"He's all right, but talks a lot and I did just wonder whether he was wanting to become a little too friendly," said Betty.

"Maybe," said Sarah. "Anyway, we'll give him a rest for the weekend – and you, too," she added. They little realised that this was not going to be so easy.

Stephen, Sarah, Gerry and John, with Betty set off quite early on Saturday morning. Their destination was the Bunya Mountains, two and a half hour's drive inland from Brisbane. The road wound up and down hills which became increasingly forested with enormous ancient bunya pine trees, strangler fig trees and thick and rich vegetation. They left the car and began to walk, while Stephen told Betty that the bunya trees produced heavy cones which could cause fatal injury if they dropped onto one's head from a height, as they weighted about ten kilos. In the more open spaces there were kangaroos and wallabies, bush turkeys and a multitude of smaller wildlife, as well as many different birds, each with a different and varied birdsong. It was a magical and amazingly interesting excursion.

They were walking alongside a stream when a loud plomp came from just behind them. It was one of the bunya pine cones that had fallen, fortunately without hitting them, but as they had all turned round, at the same moment a voice from further back along the path they had just traversed called out "Hi!"

It was Alf.

"I saw your car," he added, "and I thought I might catch you up."

They greeted him, as charitably and as politely as they could, as he walked up to join them.

"I heard you say yesterday that you'd be coming here, so thought I'd follow along. Hope you don't mind?"

Gerry and John strode on ahead. Sarah and Stephen had been there with them before, so they knew the path quite well, and they clearly were not too keen on being restricted in their explorations by adult conversation which they doubtless knew would be especially dull now that Alf had joined them.

Betty succeeded in walking alongside Sarah so that Alf would have to be with Stephen. All went well at first but it was not long before Alf had somehow managed to be level with Betty. She gave him no encouragement when he attempted to hold her hand to help her down a slightly muddy slope. She took her hand quickly and firmly away, so that Alf hopefully would get the message.

It looked as though her stay in Brisbane would not be easy if he was going to be hovering around her all the time. She would have to speak with Sarah about it.

Fortunately, Alf had not booked in at a hotel for the night, and before nightfall he left them to drive back to Brisbane. Betty breathed a sigh of relief, and that evening made it clear to the family that, while she had no wish to offend Alf or jeopardise their friendship with him, she really had no wish to go out with him again. She felt that they understood. The boys laughed, and Gerry said, "Don't worry Betty, we'll get him to take us to the cricket match here in Brisbane next week."

The rest of the weekend spent in the rain forest was full of interest for Betty as well as being relaxing. The two boys, lively as they were, nevertheless seemed to really enjoy walking about amongst the trees and undergrowth, watching the animals, and, at one point meeting up with three other youngsters, one of whom they knew from school.

Betty's thoughts frequently fell back to Edward, and how much he would have enjoyed it all. Several days later she went on her own via the City Cat to the Catholic Cathedral in the centre of Brisbane and whilst spending a while praying there she had a very strong feeling that Edward was there too and that he was speaking to her. He was telling her to enjoy her stay, but not to stay in Australia more than a few weeks and then she should return home to London.

As she sat in the vast and comparatively cool Cathedral, the presence of Edward seemed very vivid. She didn't see him, but somehow she felt his presence and, yes, she was sure she could smell the distinctive after-shave lotion he used. Was this just imagination? She had heard of people having similar experiences, and anyway she believed in a life after death, so perhaps Edward was now trying to communicate with her and advise her as he used to do. It was a strange experience. Should she act on it?

At that point a priest appeared and entered the confessional near where Betty was seated. She reflected that, while she had been to Mass quite often since Edward had died, she hadn't been to confession for many years. This would be a good opportunity and, as she sat there thinking about it, several people came up, knelt for a few minutes and then disappeared into the confessional. Betty finally plucked up courage and followed as the last one came out.

She could not remember from her childhood days what she was supposed to say and as she entered through the open door she suddenly became confused. To begin with there in front of her was a kneeler and a grille, but to the side of this was placed a chair and she saw beyond that the figure of the priest. She made a quick decision: it seemed more natural just to sit and tell the priest about herself, her regrets, her doubts and difficulties and, yes, her sins over the past years. It was such a long time since her first few confessions when she was approaching adolescence and before the family had moved. She hadn't even thought about it when she and Edward had married. They had been married in the Church of England although neither of them was a member of that church.

"Father," she began as she sat down, "it's very many years, almost a lifetime, since I went to confession so perhaps you can help me." He was immediately welcoming and sympathetic and she felt that she could open up completely to him. He listened to her attentively. "The Lord understands your situation," he said, "and he never stops loving you even when you yourself have not acted as a loving person. Continue growing in your response to his love and know that you are never alone. He is always with you and a proof of that is what you have told me about your husband's death and the prayer you read to him as he was dying. That is a wonderful sign of God's love and I am sure, if you continue to turn to him each day, you will be led to work for him in other ways that you cannot now imagine." Betty felt a great peace and calm sweep over her as he pronounced God's forgiveness and once again she felt the presence of Edward close to her. All was well.

Two more weeks passed leisurely with more outings, visits to some of Stephen and Sarah's friends and then, one Sunday, the family said they would go with her to Mass.

Stephen, like Betty, had been brought up as a Catholic but he had completely lapsed when he married Sarah who claimed to be agnostic. Philip suggested that they should go to Albany Creek church which was a half hour drive from Toowong, as some friends who also went to that church had invited them all to lunch.

This was agreed, and as they all approached the main door of the church where quite a few people had already gathered, they were welcomed first by the priest, and then by someone who seemed to be an official welcomer.

Where were they from, he enquired. "From Toowong and England."

"Ah, from England," he replied when told about Betty. "You must find the climate different here. Are you staying long?"

They chatted for a moment and then, on entering the church, which was by then nearly full, eventually found seats, and two people moved up so that the five of them could all sit together.

Betty wondered how the others would find it: Stephen who had not been to church for many years, Sarah who had never been before, and the boys who had had experiences of being at Mass at the Catholic school they attended.

It was clearly a lively parish with young families, young people, an excellent music group and an elderly but active and enthusiastic priest to whom even John and Gerry listened and later commented on a remark he had made during his homily when he had mentioned that Jesus must have had a sense of humour. Once he had said that it would be easier for a camel to pass through the eye of a needle - or since the Greek for a camel is almost the same word as for a ship's hawser, it's like saying that it's easier to thread a darning needle with a ship's cable - than for a rich man to enter the kingdom of heaven. Today, the priest had gone on to say "Jesus might well have said that it would be easier for a jumbo jet to land in the church car park than for a rich man to enter the kingdom." This had clearly impressed young Gerry, and John had actually laughed at the time.

Betty was pleased that they had all been together. Perhaps this would be the beginning of an interest in the church. Stephen remarked afterwards that there had been many changes in Catholicism since his boyhood, and he'd found it all quite interesting.

As they came out of the church several more people spoke to them, and then the family with whom they were to have lunch came over and Stephen introduced them to Betty. They were a young family with two small children aged three years and four months. The parents, Noel and Victoria Redbridge, were clearly a loving couple and welcomed Betty with a warm hug.

"Great to meet you, Betty," said Noel. "Steve and Sarah told us of your arrival. These are our two tiny ones, Hannah who stands up, and Samantha who lies down." The latter was asleep in a carrycot but Hannah was clearly becoming impatient and tugging at her Mother's hand. "She was good in church," added Victoria, but she wants us to get back home for the reward of a scoop of ice-cream!"

"Yes, ice-cream, Mom, and dampers," cried out Hannah.

With that, and a few more introductory remarks, they all made their way to the underground car park adjacent to the church, and drove off, Stephen and family following the Redbridges.

Over the lunch, which the young couple seemed to produce almost immediately on arrival, although Betty noticed that Sarah had contributed a few elements of it, the conversation turned to religion. In fact it was young John who introduced the subject by asking why there were candles in the church and why the priest wore a coloured skirt.

Betty was trying to think of a quick and accurate answer but breathed relief when Noel said: "Candles used to be the only source of light when Christians worshipped in the catacombs in Rome – they are underground caves where the followers of Jesus used to hide when they were being persecuted by the pagan Romans, and the special clothes the priest wears date also from that time when it was the normal everyday gear. Now we dress differently, but these old customs remind us of the fact that the church goes way back to the time of Christ."

By this time John seemed to have almost lost interest, but his older brother had been following and asked, "But why do people go to church?" How was that going to be answered, wondered Betty. Noel, however, seemed quite up to it.

"Very briefly," he said, "Jesus, who was God, became one of us to show us that God is love, got together a group of people whom he taught how to pray and to live properly, and he sent them off to tell others all about this good news. And then, just before he was put to death, he had a very special meal with some of his followers and told them that he would rise from the dead and be present to them whenever they repeated this special meal. In fact he said that he would be present under the form of the bread and wine which they were to eat and drink."

"Gosh, that was extraordinary!" exclaimed Gerry.

"Yes, continued Noel, "and that is what we now call the Mass or the Eucharist, which is a Greek word meaning thanksgiving."

Sarah and Stephen had been listening with interest during all this.

"Noel, you explained that jolly well," said Stephen. "It brought back the memory of things I'd learned at school."

"And no longer practise!" Betty could not refrain from adding, although she felt slightly hypocritical as she hadn't in the past practised her faith.

"Well, it's not all that easy," countered Stephen. "There are so many pressures in life today. However, I must say that the boys do well at their Catholic school. Perhaps we'll all have to go to church sometimes."

"Yes, you're always welcome to come here with us, but first of all," said Noel, "it must be a matter of faith: belief in God, belief that, as I said just now, God came amongst us, and belief in the Church that he founded."

At this point Sarah chipped in, "It all sounds quite simple, and I thought Catholicism was so complex."

"It's summed up in the word 'love'," Betty replied. "Love: God's love of us and our love of God and of one another. I know that's helped me these past months since Edward died. I really couldn't have gone on without some faith."

"And you really believe that Edward is still alive?" asked Sarah.

"Yes, more alive than he was before. The resurrection of Jesus guarantees that. I'm really convinced of that through an experience I had the other day when I was in the Cathedral." She then recounted what had happened to her whilst she was praying.

"That could have been imagination," said Stephen.

"But I know that it wasn't," his sister replied. At that point Noel turned to their baby who had begun to awaken. She had been quiet up to that point. Victoria said, "She thinks we're becoming very serious and…."

She was interrupted by Gerry, who asked, "I'd like to know why at the end of the service we prayed for an end to the drought." Brisbane and its surroundings had been suffering from the worst drought in living memory and every Sunday the congregation in all churches had been praying for rain. Occasionally, there had been a few heavy downfalls but it had failed to fall over the reservoirs and these were becoming sadly depleted of water. Someone had remarked that he could easily imagine Australia being a desert in a few decades time.

"God could do something about this, couldn't he? Why doesn't he?" said Gerry. It was clearly for Noel to reply.

"That's a very good question," he replied. "To begin with," he continued, "we have to remember that God has made our universe will all the laws of nature, but he's not like a great magician waiting ready to act against those laws whenever something goes wrong, like the tsunami which killed so many people the other year, and the various earthquakes we often hear about. Some disasters are man-made – man misusing his freedom, but some natural disasters like the drought may or may not be due to man's wrong use of his freewill. And then good can come from natural disasters and from evil in general, even from the suffering of the innocent. Jesus, who was totally innocent, showed this by his death and resurrection."

"That demands faith," interrupted Sarah.

"Yes, it does," Noel replied, "and it means we have to be aware of God loving us. The trouble today is that, for the most part, we hear only the bad news, the negative happenings. People seem attracted to hearing about bad things. Good news is no news. You know, some years ago, there was a national appeal for 80,000 people to subscribe to a daily newspaper that highlighted good news instead of the evil and which would run for three years. Insufficient names were put forward and so the paper never got printed."

"It's all a big question – and something of a mystery," remarked Stephen.

"I want to go for a swim," chimed in John. "Can I Dad?"

"In another half an hour," replied his father. "When your lunch has settled."

With that the serious discussion that had developed was concluded and they all agreed that it was time to relax, swim, read or help Noel and Victoria clear away.

For Betty it had been a very pleasant day, and she was pleased to be with this clearly very committed Christian family.

She had not joined in the religious discussion, but had listened with interest. It had caused her to reflect on Edward's illness, and the evil of cancer and why he had died. What good would come of that? When she had gone to confession she recalled how the priest had ended by saying that she would be led to work for God in ways she couldn't now begin to imagine.

What good was she supposed to bring out of it? What work did God want of her? How was she to occupy her time now that, once back in England, she was going to be living on her own? These were so far unanswered questions.

The days passed rapidly for her. She got to know Brisbane well, at least the city centre and the attractive conglomerate of shops in the Mall. She also came to know and appreciate Sarah and the two boys. Both of them liked to ask her all sorts of questions about England, and London in particular. She was reminded that Sarah, when she was eighteen, had lived for a while in London before she returned to Australia, where she was born, and that she had had a brief affair with a young marine. Unbeknown to her parents, who had remained in Sydney, she had become pregnant, had a child, a boy, whom she had had adopted through an agency. Stephen knew about it. She had told him soon after they had met on her return to Australia and when she took up work in an office in Brisbane. She confided in Betty that she had often wondered what had become of the boy. By now he would be over twenty-one years of age. At times the thought of her unknown son haunted her, and she was afraid of speaking about it to Stephen.

"Do you know his adoptive parents?" Betty asked her.

"Yes, I know where they used to be, but I don't know whether the adoption agency would have kept track of them."

Betty was sympathetic and felt for the dilemma Sarah was experiencing.

"If I could do anything to help when I return to England, and if you'd like me to, then I'll certainly do my best."

"That would be really great," answered Sarah. It was then that Betty began to think of her return journey. She had an open ticket, and she decided to make arrangements to return the following week.

When the time came, she felt sad and bewildered. What was awaiting her? What was she going to do? How was she to occupy her time? She felt only very slightly more sure of herself and how she was to cope. Perhaps she would get involved in some sort of church work, and then she would certainly try to track down Sarah's son. That would be a challenge for her. However, on reflection, she felt it was important for Sarah to tell Stephen what she was doing.

The time came for Betty to leave and all the family took her to the airport. To Betty's amazement Alf also turned up just as she was checking in her bags. She had not seen him since the day they had all gone to the Bunya mountains. He was quite affable and spoke most of the time with Sarah and Stephen whilst they were waiting.

As Sarah gave Betty a warm hug she whispered "I've told Stephen what you're going to try to do, and he's O.K. about it."

They all bade her fond farewells with the two boys promising to go to see her in London when they were a little older. As yet they knew nothing of the possible existence of a half-brother.

The flight was uneventful. When, quite weary after twenty-four hours in the air, to say nothing of the two changes and various minor delays, she walked past the arrival barrier and knew there would be no one to meet her, a sudden wave of deep loneliness swept over her. She was going to miss the family and friends in Australia.

Her first days after her return were busy. She made contact with various friends she knew, as well as Edward's former colleagues from work. There was some business to attend to regarding Edward's will. And then she would see about trying to trace Sarah's son.

His first name was Gordon but Sarah had thought that he would have taken his adopted parents surname. Betty had to find this from the adoption agency. She had Sarah's written authority to make the necessary enquiries. It was going to be good keeping herself occupied, and this was particularly important as the evenings were still dark and the house was so empty without Edward there.

It was several weeks later that she heard from the adoption agency that the name of the couple who had adopted Gordon was Greenford and that they lived, or at least used to live, in West Ruislip. She was unable to find the name Greenford in that area, so she decided that the best plan was to visit the address the agency had given her and maybe the new occupants of the house could help.

She took the Central Line tube without much difficulty and found the address which was a large semi-detached house with big bay windows. She rang the bell and was immediately answered by a loud barking from within.

Above the sound of the barking dog a woman's voice called out "Ben, Ben, here….here, Sit." The door opened and a tall thin lady with a somewhat severe face stood there. Judging by her expression, Betty surmised that she had either been asleep or watching the television.

"I do apologise for having disturbed you," began Betty, "but I have called on the off-chance of finding a Mr & Mrs Greenford."

"Yes," replied the lady at the door. "What can I do for you? I am Mrs Greenford."

"Well, it's quite a delicate matter, really, so would you mind if I came in for a moment?" said Betty, and she added, "I should introduce myself: I am Betty Snaresbrook and my brother is married to Sarah, who before she married, was Sarah Roding."

This last brought no reaction from Mrs Greenford, who merely said rather reluctantly, "Come in", and led the way into a darkened room in which the television was switched on but was yielding no sound. Betty could just make out a settee and two armchairs, over one was strewn a rug and several extra cushions. A large bookcase stood in one corner and as she became accustomed to the lack of light she realised that the room was comfortably furnished with an ornate coffee table and several classical oil paintings, albeit reproductions, on the walls. There was one cabinet with glass shelves full of small silver ornaments, jugs and what looked like surgical instruments.

All this Betty took in at a glance in spite of the dim light, whilst Mrs Greenford said, "Oh, do sit down – and what can I do for you?"

She was some years younger than Betty and her long swept-up hair seemed to add to her superior air. Betty became hesitant, wondering what sort of reaction she would get from this somewhat autocratic lady. She continued: "Recently I was staying with my brother in Australia and was talking to his wife who told me that, before she was married to my brother, she had a son who was adopted. She had not met the adoptive parents and did not know their name, but she often thought of this son, whose name was Gordon....."

At this Mrs Greenford suddenly looked startled. "My son is adopted – but he doesn't know it – and his name is Gordon," said Mrs Greenford. The haughtiness seemed to have gone from her voice as she said this. "How old would this Gordon be?" she asked softly.

"About twenty-one," said Betty.

"My Gordon is turned twenty. We adopted him when he was only six weeks old. My husband has his birth certificate locked up somewhere, and I don't remember the surname on it, but he took our name, of course." She paused for a moment and then added, "We're not going to lose him now, you know; and anyway as far as he knows, we are his real parents."

"No. I don't think there need be any fear of that," said Betty. "His real mother just wanted to know if he was alive and well, and......well, just some news of him."

"So long as she doesn't want him back," said Mrs Greenford again. Then she stood, thoughtfully, "We've both thought that we'd have to tell him sometime soon that he's adopted, but it won't be easy – perhaps more difficult now."

"That needn't be so," replied Betty. "I presume he's living here with you."

"Oh yes, but at the moment he is away on a course, and I'm not sure when he'll be back, but he'll ring up probably some time tonight. "

"Do tell me what you can about him," said Betty. "My sister-in-law would really like to know, but I do promise you that she would not contact him if you didn't wish it. She just wants reassurance that he's alive, being looked after well and is happy." Then, after a pause, she added, "Of course, if you were in agreement, she could perhaps write to him, but that would only be "if", and "when", you told him that he was adopted."

"Well, perhaps," replied Mrs Greenford, "but I'll have to speak to my husband about it, and then I'll let you know."

They continued to talk and Mrs Greenford, whose first name Betty learned was Alice, made some tea. Meanwhile, Betty learned quite a lot about Gordon. In the course of the conversation Alice provided a fairly recent photo of him and Betty was struck by the resemblance to his natural mother, Sarah. She also thought she had seen him somewhere, but couldn't think where.

"I'll give you another photo similar to this one," said Alice, "and you can send it to Sarah, but," she added once again, "don't do that until we've spoken with Gordon and that won't be for a few weeks when he returns from his holiday. "

Just as Betty eventually got up to leave, she noticed a photograph on the wall behind the chair where she had been seated. It was a photo of a man and a woman, the latter being seated whilst the man stood half behind her.

Although taken some years previously, Betty immediately recognised the woman as Alice. The man she was with she also recognised. It was none other than the doctor to whom Edward and she used to go and who had told them of the seriousness of Edward's condition. But then, how could it be? His name was Dr Farthing?

She was about to go out of the door when the dog suddenly appeared on the scene again and, whilst Alice was trying to restrain it, Betty had time to remark, "That's a good photo of you, and I presume your husband?"

"Yes, that's Peter."

"He reminds me very much of my doctor at Notting Hill, but his name is Farthing."

"That's my husband," replied Alice "You see, when we married, we decided to go under my family name of Greenford. I wasn't happy with his surname as it was open to all sorts of crude jokes, but Peter had already been in practice for six years and had got quite used to having his leg pulled about his name, and amongst his fellow practitioners he was always known as "Farts". I wanted him to change, but I think he also felt a certain loyalty to his family. However, Gordon, of course, took the name of Greenford."

"How extraordinary! What a coincidence," exclaimed Betty, "that I should know your husband."

"Yes," said Alice, "it's a small world. Well, goodbye. I have your address and phone number and I'll have a chat with Peter about it all."

It was at least three weeks later that Betty received a phone call from Alice Greenford. She had been wondering how to find an excuse to make an appointment to see Dr

Farthing in order to open up the subject of Gordon with him, but had refrained from doing so. At last Alice had phoned and told her that Gordon had returned home and she and Peter had had the difficult task of telling him that they were not his real parents. He seemed to have taken it very well, and had asked a lot of questions about his natural parents. Alice had suggested that he had a talk with Betty. This was duly arranged and Betty went once again to the address in Ruislip to meet Gordon.

Peter and Alice had invited her for dinner one evening. Once again Betty was more than ever struck by the likeness to Sarah.

The evening was spent talking about Betty's brother and sister-in-law and Gordon wanted to know a lot about his mother and his half-brothers. Would they ever meet? He would certainly like to, but, he added, he'd most of all like to meet his mother.

"But you'll always regard us as your parents," Alice interrupted at this point.

"Of course, Mother," said Gordon. "You've both done so much for me. I suppose it's curiosity and some sort of blood tie that must be there, but it doesn't mean that my tie with you will ever be broken. No fear of that," and he said this clearly with heartfelt conviction. The evening passed quickly and, with Alice and Peter's approval, Betty said that she would send to Sarah and tell her and Stephen all the news, and send Gordon's photograph.

Several weeks later and arising from this, Gordon made contact with his mother and half-brothers and, by means of the internet and an occasional telephone conversation, a firm bonding developed between the two families.

The following year Stephen, Sarah and the boys decided to take a holiday in Europe. It was to be a package tour from Rome, via Florence, Venice, Lucerne and Paris to London, where they planned to stay with Betty for a few days and to meet Gordon. Unfortunately, they had planned this holiday at the same time that Gordon had already arranged to be in Turkey. Thus it transpired that there was only one day when Sarah and the family could see him before they returned to Brisbane.

Betty arranged for them all, including Gordon's adoptive parents, Peter and Alice, to meet at her house, where she had gone to considerable trouble to prepare a meal for them all. There were eight altogether – Sarah and Stephen, the two boys John and Gerry, Peter and Alice, Gordon's adoptive parents, Gordon, and of course, Betty.

It was an emotional meeting, especially between Sarah and Gordon. Peter and Alice were apprehensive about the outcome, still fearing that they might lose Gordon, although they realised that he was now a grown man in his twenties. Betty busied herself with the cooking and serving whilst the others began to talk. The tears were slowly coursing down Sarah's cheeks as she looked at Gordon, who seemed to be equally moved. Peter and Alice were holding hands and looking on a little fearfully whilst the two boys, who were with Stephen, glanced across the room at Gordon, and John called out, "Say, you're our brother!" "Half-brother," corrected Gerry.

The initial emotions subsided, the fears of Alice and Peter abated and all became engaged in lively conversation about their lives, about Brisbane and about London, until the time came for the Australian contingent to depart and prepare for their flight home.

Tears and smiles came to the fore when finally they all dispersed except for Gordon who lingered behind. "Betty," he turned to her, "I can't say how much I appreciate what you've done for me. It's so extraordinary how it's all worked out and I'm really most grateful. My adoptive parents have taken it so well, too. Thanks so much," and he gave her a great hug. He then became thoughtful for a moment. "Tomorrow," he said, "I'm going on a sort of mission to a place I've never heard of before. If you're not busy, and you'd like a day out, I'd be very happy if you'd come along too." He then proceeded to tell her about an old Irishman he and his friend Andrew had met and of how, when in Turkey, they'd been given his notebook and a message about going to Eziat.

"That sounds interesting," replied Betty. "Yes, I'd be pleased to come with you."

They arranged to meet the following morning to go to Eziat. It was the twentieth of June and just three years to the day that both, unbeknown to the other, had been on the same Central Line train that had been held up in the tunnel. Betty was the first to recall this when she remarked that she hoped there wouldn't be another delay, not that it mattered so much this time as they hadn't to keep an appointment with Dr Farthing.

"No, but it's very odd," said Gordon, "that it's exactly three years to the day that we were on this same train, little knowing how our lives would, as it were, intertwine." He little knew how extensive the intertwining was. This they were both to discover later in the day.

Chapter 6 – The Pythagorean Cup

Philip Leyton would have described himself as a prosperous business man, the managing director of a London firm specialising in the design of websites. His main office was in the city, but Philip often worked from home, travelling just two or three times a week into London and sometimes to various branches in other parts of Europe.

He lived with Agnes, his wife, and two teenage daughters in a spacious house overlooking Ealing Common. His wife, Agnes, was an extravagant woman who spent a lot, not only on clothes for herself but she frequently purchased new items for the home. This was lavishly furnished with hand-woven Turkish carpets, beautifully draped velvet curtains, several china, glass and silver cabinets, three long-case clocks, antique uncomfortable chairs and the walls concealed by a miscellany of oil paintings, some originals and others reproductions. Philip had accepted all this, feeling that he was obliged to indulge his wife in this way. She herself objected to what she termed his meanness and had recently told him that she was thinking of leaving him.

He had a small room at the top of the house where he worked when at home. However, whilst his material surroundings were almost ideal, his relationship with his wife was not, and his two daughters invariably sided with their mother if there was any discussion about what to spend money on. This was the usual topic of disagreement.

So it was that in the summer of 2005 he had begun to feel the need to get away from home and reflect a little on his whole situation, in particular his marriage.

His thoughts were turned in this direction one morning when he was travelling to the city. The train was held up owing to an accident at Queensway and everyone had to get out of the packed train. Philip was almost the last and he had noticed next to him a young man with an overfull rucksack which bore a label with the man's name and the one word "Corsica". For Philip at that moment this word and the sight of the rucksack spelt out freedom and leisure and time to think. It also took him back to holidays he had enjoyed in his youth. Now he had been married for nearly twenty years and he felt an increasing need to think about his relationship, indeed to escape from it for at least a while.

These thoughts filled his mind as he changed trains and went on to his office. By lunchtime he had decided to go to a nearby travel agent and arrange his escape. He could tell his wife what he was going to do after he'd made definite bookings.

Corsica did not interest him, but islands did: a small quiet Greek Island somewhere would be ideal. By evening he had booked to stay in a hotel on a tiny island off Rhodes. Unfortunately, he was unable to arrange it until towards the end of August. However, the decision was made and it was booked and he could wait. When he returned home and told his wife she seemed almost pleased. "That's good," she had said.

Thus it was that on the 29th of August Philip was standing on the lower deck of a ferry boat taking him on the hour and a half journey across from Rhodes to the island of

Halki. It was approaching darkness and the island was revealing itself as a great black shadow with tiny twinkling lights near its base and to which the boat was heading. He had waited two months for this and now it had begun. Next to him stood another passenger with whom he had passed a few cursory remarks. She too was from England, travelling with two friends. However, she explained, they preferred to remain in the inside lounge whilst she wanted to see the setting sun.

Then, just as they were each enjoying the still calm sea and the sight of the sun disappearing below the clear straight line of the horizon, Philip felt moisture wetting his bare arms as he leaned against the wooden rail of the side of the boat. "It surely can't be raining," he remarked to the lady. "Nor can it be spray," he added.

"I felt something, too," replied the other.

Philip glanced up, and there leaning over the rail of the deck above them was the dark face of a Greek woman who had, in spite of the calm sea, felt suddenly ill and had taken the shortest route to venting her inner feelings!

Philip and his travelling companion made their way to the toilet where Philip had to wash and don a clean tee-shirt and shorts, all of which were spattered with the woman's sickness. This, he thought, was a good introduction to his holiday!

The peace and solitude he had hoped for was shattered to a far greater degree when the boat eventually, by then in darkness, docked in at the harbour. He had landed on the night of the great island feast, St John the Baptist. The harbour itself, normally very quiet, was full of sound and movement. A group of three musicians with stringed instruments were leading the dancing of the crowd gathering there, some dressed in gaily coloured national costume. Others were seated at tables eating and drinking. Philip found his way to the small hotel where he had reserved a room. It was at one end of the harbour but as the harbour curved round, it was almost opposite the site of the festivities, which, in spite of his tiredness after the journey, he heard intermittently until nearly six o'clock in the morning.

He found out later that, in addition to the two hundred residents of Halki, others who had been born there usually returned for the feast from Rhodes, Athens, or even as far as Australia and America to which they had emigrated. Some of these had founded a sponge diving community in Florida, had become comparatively rich and returned to build a concrete road, named Tarpen Springs Boulevard, leading from the harbour village to the original capital, Chorio, now in ruins just below the similarly ruined Crusader castle.

After his sleepless night and a leisurely breakfast, Philip nevertheless felt energised and decided to walk up to the ruined castle which was perched higher on the steepest part of the hilly island. He stopped on the way and found a small taverna set by a stretch of sandy beach. Some of the fifty or so people sunning themselves or swimming in the shallow sea were mostly visitors to the island, with a few who were Greek. He sat at a table overlooking the beach sipping his iced lager and watching three elderly ladies who had come down fully clad, two with wider brimmed dark straw hats and the third with a shawl tied round her head. She had a stick and had difficulty walking, probably due to an arthritic hip.

All three had then proceeded to remove their black dresses revealing long almost white petticoats, dating, on modern standards, to a style of some forty years earlier. The one with the arthritic hip had laid her towel, her dress and a bag on the beach very near the water's edge, and had then hobbled hesitantly into the water. The other two kept quite near her. However, she had no sooner got into the water until it was up to her waist when a sudden great gust of wind blew her dress into the water as well. She managed to reach out for it, and seemingly unperturbed, struggled back to the beach and laid the dress on the sand to dry. Back she then went into the sea, but with just her feet and ankles under water, one hand disappeared under her petticoat where she seemed to be searching somewhere in those female regions normally hidden from sight, until she extracted from under the bottom of the petticoat a black bra which she threw onto the sand also to dry. Finally satisfied, she limped into deeper water and began gently to move her arms in a semicircular fashion, the lower part of her body well below the surface so that all that could be seen was her head and a black straw hat bobbing in the water.

Philip had been fascinated by this spectacle. He was enjoying being alone, and he enjoyed the quiet, almost contemplative, silence that seemed to permeate the whole island. Just looking and listening. This was in contrast to the previous night. He recalled how he and Agnes had spent a holiday two years previously on another Greek island, but it had been far from quiet. They had stayed in a self-catering flat in the main street of the small town of Spetses. Philip had decided that the local Greek population had no need of television, telephone or radio, as their voices, especially the female ones, were loud, raucous, piercing and penetrating. They even competed well with the noise of motor cycles and mopeds speeding up and down the narrow winding streets.

In the late evenings, the men ruled supreme in the cafés, their conversation continuing well into the night. This, Philip decided, was the Greek form of family planning! Often the local Orthodox priest would be there too and he would join in with what often sounded like a violent argument, but it usually seemed to conclude quite amicably.

On one occasion the sound of human voices merged with that of a few solitary cockerels prematurely doing their dawn duty. These were joined later by donkeys and dogs, and not long after this with the noise of the water in the pipes from the neighbours' flat where the occupants were trying unsuccessfully to have a shower from a blocked shower spray. Even two years previously he recalled that this had caused tension between Agnes and himself.

Leaving the beach and the three elderly ladies who were still flapping about in the water, he continued his walk up the steep hill towards the ruined castle. A gentle gust of wind in the trees, the distant sound of a great bell and nearby the buzz of flies around the prickly shrubs almost harmonising with the far off hum of an outboard motor out at sea, was all that he could hear. For the rest just a deep stillness. This was what he had craved for - in order to think - to think out his problems.

He climbed through the ruined village until he came to the castle. It was perched high with pretty well impregnable battlements. Philip looked down through the clear air to the coast far below and an isthmus where just three women were enjoying the solitude of a small patch of sandy beach. Hundreds of dragonflies were spinning around and enjoying the sunshine and the clear unpolluted air. As he looked he thought he saw one of the three on the beach look up towards him. He thought she waved, but it was so far down and the three figures seemed but tiny specks. He was not sure, but he thought it might have been the lady with whom he had spoken on the boat, so to be on the safe side, he returned the wave. There was nothing to lose, or to gain, by a friendly gesture at that distance. Then he thought, but how could one possibly be sure in that situation, that it was the same one. Perhaps............but so what?

He continued to absorb the still clear atmosphere around the castle before investigating further. As he looked at the somewhat scant ruins of the Knights of St John Crusader castle, he recalled how bloodthirsty and cruel human beings could be to one another – all in the name of religion. Some years previously he had visited another such castle also built by the Crusaders in another Greek island. There he had been shown the former banqueting hall which had three trap doors situated in the floor beneath the long banqueting table. He was told by the guide that after the meal, the table was cleared, the trap doors opened, and the scraps of food left over were swept into the holes in the floor to be consumed by the prisoners captured by the Crusaders, who were kept there in complete darkness for several weeks until they slowly starved and died.

Halki, Philip decided, was so different. It seemed to be pervaded by peace. It was just unfortunate that he had arrived on the night of the fiesta. However, the following night after his walk to the castle, proved to be different. He had looked out at the dark sky and, as his eyes grew accustomed to the blackness, he discerned the irregular pattern of tiny twinkling stars. It was an incredibly peaceful and restful experience and was broken just occasionally by the soft chugging or softly splashing paddle of a small fishing boat approaching its mooring near the welcoming lights of the quayside.

Halki was rapidly growing on him. It was such a complete contrast to Ealing and underground trains and work in the office, but, most of all, he was enjoying the solitude and being away from stress and tension and arguments.

The next day he decided to extend his walk by going as far as the monastery which was near the far end of the island. He set off early to avoid the midday heat. He would be alone. This was what he wanted. It was a two and a half hour walk, mostly uphill, and he met only one local farmer on a donkey, laden with hay and sacks of figs and fruit. As he climbed he became increasingly aware of the clear pure air, which once again, he compared with the pollution he was used to in London.

The rough track that had replaced the road on the last part of his walk was punctuated at intervals by patches of burnt shrubbery which had been caused by the small fires lit two days earlier to mark the island's feast of St John the Baptist. After their celebrations in the village, many would have journeyed late at night to the monastery and there would have venerated the icon of St John whose head was seen resting on a plate.

Entering the church he looked at the icon with some horror. Man's cruelty to man. It had hardly changed. No sooner had Philip come out of the church where he was glad to have sat down in the comparative cool, than a man in his thirties came from one of the buildings and introduced himself as Demetrius. Immediately his wife and two children, a boy aged five and his sister aged eight, joined him and set a cup of hot coffee and pieces of chopped cucumber and bread in front of Philip. Four others, people who turned out to be visiting relatives, also seated themselves by Philip. Unfortunately, Demetrius' knowledge of English was about the equivalent of Philip's Greek; just five or six words. Nevertheless a certain basic communication ensued and Philip gathered that the two children travelled down to the port village to school by donkey every day. This was no mean feat, considering that it had taken Philip two and a half hours to walk up to the monastery. Demetrius' father, who had also looked after the monastery after the monks had left, used to walk to the village barefoot. Philip found the simplicity of the life of this family both inspiring and thought-provoking. It was so completely different from the life he himself was used to – and these people seemed so happy. He felt once again the need to sort himself out.

His wife, Agnes, had several times hinted at a divorce and she had clearly been pleased at the thought of his going away for a week. Their marriage had just turned out to be that of two incompatible people, and probably the fact that he was working from home much of the time hadn't helped. They saw too much of each other. He was invariably there when she returned from her extravagant shopping expeditions....and the two girls were taking after their mother.

After further exchanges of conversation, both verbal and in signs, Philip finally left Demetrius and his family and relatives and set off on the walk back to the village. By the time he arrived at the harbour front, he noticed two bronzed young Greeks unravelling their nets ready to set off again that evening. Others were ensconced in hard wicker chairs sipping their ouzo or playing backgammon in one of the nearby cafes.

After a cool shower and a short rest, Philip decided to eat out and after viewing several harbourside restaurants, he settled on one where an old man, presumably the owner, smiled and beckoned him to sit down. Several other visitors were already seated.

The old man had to descend eight stone steps to get to the level of the tables as the ground rose steeply behind the restaurant, and clearly, the kitchen and other facilities were on the higher level. There seemed to be no set menu, which was perhaps as well for Philip had been slightly put off by one menu he had seen which included "steak of veals, intestines, Boorish salad and Goat in tomatoe sauce."

The old man proceeded to anchor a half-folded plastic cloth over the table leaving it drooping untidily on one side. This was followed by a plate of green beans which turned out to be not unlike pieces of old rope. Further dishes of pork, spaghetti, tomato and cheese were placed before Philip. The first course had been tepid but the second course was quite cold. However, Philip knew that one seldom had hot food in Greece.

Those at the other tables were enduring similar treatment, some being amused whilst others seemed disgruntled. A French couple who had been cycling had obviously considered the local wine to be inferior to the French, or perhaps because they wished to remain sober, asked for some water. The old man responded to this request by going to an enormous plane tree near the side of the restaurant and to everyone's amazement filled two glasses from a metal pipe poking out of the trunk of the tree.

At one point he nearly slipped on the steps and Philip leaped up and offered to help him down with some of the food. Immediately he was handed a plate of Greek salad, and the old man followed this by stuffing a pepper pot in the pocket of Philip's shirt and a further hunk of bread under his arm. There seemed to be no one else to help with the serving and Philip guessed that he probably prepared all the food himself. However, to investigate this would certainly have been unwise.

Philip was getting to know parts of the island quite well so the following day he decided to set off in the opposite direction, to the east. It was not as hilly and he walked past a cluster of blue-painted bee-hives, a pile of old car-tyres probably dumped by the restaurant owners who seemed to be the only owners of the island's four-wheeled vehicles, and then on beyond to a tiny wayside shrine. Approaching the sea, he clambered over bare rocks, through clumps of prickly foliage towards a small patch of sandy beach. He noticed a smell of decaying flesh. It was probably, he thought, a dead donkey or goat rotting away.

That was like an image of his marriage. His love seemed dead. Then he saw the dead animal. It was the carcase of a goat lying near the low bush, fortunately far enough from the patch of sand not to upset him.

Arrived at the patch of sand, which could hardly be called a beach in the tradition of Nice or the idyllic locations he had in the past visited with his wife, he stretched himself out with his head resting where the sand gave way to stones and boulders and with his feet almost wet from the gently lapping waves. If anyone had wished to walk past they would have had to step over him. However he felt fairly certain that no one would come that way.

He watched the birds zooming in and out of the crevices between some nearby rocks. He gazed at the calm water gently splashing his feet. He thought of war and man wanting to capture land from others. It made no sense. Man could never possess the land. It was God's land, God's earth, and we were all tenants. He wasn't particularly religious but he did believe in God. It just didn't make sense to spoil the world, to mutilate it, to pollute it, nor to try to possess it. He then began to think, once again, of his own life. Agnes, his wife, seemed continually to be wanting to possess things, objects, clothes, furniture, yes, and even himself. That was one of the problems. That was why he had to escape and be alone for a while.

It was so quiet and peaceful. It seemed that no one could possibly venture to this secluded spot. Philip decided to strip down and enjoy the freedom and sensation of the sun on his naked body. He lay there for an hour or so, having occasional five minute swims in the blue translucent water, when he thought he heard a footstep behind him. "Perhaps it was a local Greek shepherd," he thought, and so he'd best pull on his swimming trunks. "And even," it flashed through his mind, "if it were another visitor like himself, he'd best make some semblance of covering up." Germans or Scandinavians wouldn't think anything of it, but the Japanese - and there was a couple he had seen the other day – would be shocked to see a naked man sprawled out on the sand. Another English person would probably show a mixture of shock, surprise and even envy.

He had read somewhere that British tourists were officially considered the worst-behaved, the most linguistically incompetent and the least adventurous in the world. He felt he would hardly fall into any of these categories – so all was well.

Whilst these thoughts sped through his mind, he tried to extract his swimming trunks from the pocket of his shorts which he had folded and placed on the rock behind him. As he attempted to do this the visitor became visible only a few metres from the shore. It was a woman and, clearly not Greek. She had thick, short straight ginger hair, with a fringe, and was wearing white shorts and a pale blue cotton blouse through which could be detected the dark outline of her swimming costume. She wore dark glasses and Philip was unable to see what her initial reaction was on seeing him.

She stopped and, after a slight hesitation, exclaimed, "Oh, I'm sorry- I'll find another beach further along." He then realised that it was the same person with whom he'd chatted on the boat deck coming to Halki.

"Er, no," replied Philip, "I don't mind company – that is if you don't mind. I'll just put my trunks on," he added. "I was in fact just about to."

"Oh, don't worry: I've seen lots of men like that," she replied, and followed this remark by seating herself on a nearby rock.

There was a softness and gentleness about her, and yet a firmness in her voice as of one who was used to making decisions. She wore a ring on the third finger of her left hand. All this Philip noticed in an instant as she sat down. She removed her sunglasses and as she looked down at Philip there was a glint of amusement in her expression. She wore no make-up, but her complexion and features could hardly have been enhanced by it anyway.

"It looks as though we had a similar idea coming to this quiet out of the way spot," she remarked. "Have you been here before?" she added.

"No," rejoined Philip, "I spotted it on the map and decided to explore. It was quite a rough walk, wasn't it?" He looked at her flimsy beach sandals. "I'm Philip.............Philip Leyton. Where have you come from?" he added.

"Well, I am Agnes Stratford," she replied, "and at the moment I'm living in London, but originally, I'm from Ireland."

She added the last item of information as if she in no way wished to be taken for a Londoner, or perhaps to explain the slight roundness of her vowels which Philip had begun to notice.

Agnes was about Philip's age and he was beginning to sense that here was someone with whom he could talk, and with whom he really wanted to talk and unburden some of his thoughts and the difficulties he'd recently been experiencing at home. Perhaps this was in part due to the fact that he had already spent three days more or less on his own, apart from a few superficial exchanges with others in the hotel bar.

160

There was something attractive and inviting about Agnes. She exuded a warmth and a feeling of compassion and caring. Furthermore, she seemed not to be embarrassed at talking with a stranger lying naked on a secluded foreign beach. But then, thought Philip, she had hinted that she was not unfamiliar with the naked male body. Perhaps she'd had many male friends. This would not have surprised him. Was she married? Philip began to be curious.

"Are you staying here for long?" she continued.

"Do you mean on this island, or here on the beach?" countered Philip.

"On Halki," she smiled.

"Just four more days," Philip replied, "and then back to work: setting up websites for computer addicts."

"That must be one of the increasing number of occupations that can be done from home," she remarked.

"Yes, I work from home most of the time."

"And your wife as well?" she continued.

Why had she asked that, thought Philip. Well, he'd best answer honestly.

"I think I'm moving towards a divorce," he replied, "at least my wife wants to divorce me."

Immediately Agnes added, "I'm sorry to hear that, and I shouldn't have asked you, but I somehow suspected that you were going through a difficult time. I can often sense these things."

Memories and emotions connected with his past suddenly flooded into Philip. Dreams of the future and questions as to what his life was really all about surged up in his mind. Yes, he wanted to talk. He needed to talk, and he, on the spur of the moment, felt that he wanted to talk to this stranger whom he'd only just met – and in what a strange and unusual situation.

The shade from a stunted olive tree had fallen across Philip but Agnes was still seated in the warm afternoon sun. Philip decided to pull on his shorts and tee-shirt.

"Do talk if you feel you'd like to," said Agnes after a few moments. "If not," she added, "I can read my book or go for a swim." She had discerned his need.

"It's strange, you know," said Philip after a moment, "my wife's name is also Agnes – but you're not at all like her. She is................oh, well, yes," he hesitated and then said, "Yes, I'd like to tell you about her, if you really feel like listening."

He then proceeded to pour out the story of his traumatic marriage to Agnes and how he felt he had failed to satisfy her imperious needs and demands. She was crazy about clothes, always looking for a new fashion and spending hours in Paris at Christian Dior's; and then if it wasn't clothes, she would be continually re-arranging the perfectly good furniture in the home and then substituting it for the latest luxurious item offered by Harrods. If all this left time, there would invariably be evenings when she would have booked tickets in the stalls of some London theatre for herself and a certain girl friend.

Meanwhile the children, Maura sixteen years and Petina who was fourteen years, would be left to themselves, or more frequently, would be dependent on their father, Philip. They would also be witness to the habitually heated arguments between their parents. These would invariably centre on money and the accusation that Philip had no ambition to climb up the ladder of success, to earn more, and to be acclaimed by all, in spite of the fact that he already had a very good and remunerative job.

"This was all true," added Philip, at the end of his confession of his marital plight.

"I'm the sort of person who is quite content to jog along, and I do earn more than sufficient to provide for the children, my wife and myself, but that is not enough for her." He paused, "I had to come away for a few days, to be alone, to think, to decide whether it would be best to leave Agnes.............but then there were the children to consider...........I just don't know." He turned to look at Agnes, "Why am I here? Here on this earth, I mean. What should I be doing? What is life really about?"

Then he added in a strong firm voice, "Do you know what the answer to that is?"

Agnes smiled: a gentle, understanding smile as she slowly and thoughtfully replied: "I think I have some idea, but I believe that question cannot be answered without reference to God."

"So what would you say?" said Philip, clearly wishing to pursue the point further.

"I would say," continued Agnes, " that the only thing that gives meaning to our lives is loving and being loved, loving God and knowing that we are loved by him, and then loving other people and being loved by them. I've found that makes sense in my own life."

"What do you do, then?" asked Philip, hesitantly. "I've been talking a great deal about myself, perhaps because I've never really opened up to anyone who's a good listener like you. But you've not told me anything about yourself."

"Well," replied Agnes quietly and with an almost concealed twinkle in her eye, "I should perhaps tell you that I am a religious sister, a nun!"

"A nun!" Philip almost shouted it out across the gently lapping waves. "My last encounter with a nun was on a previous Greek island holiday soon after Agnes and I were married. It was on Tinos, noted for its pigeons and pious people." Philip's thoughts immediately took him back those fifteen years to his experience of black-habited and somewhat severe-looking Greek Orthodox nuns slowly on their knees ascending the steps to the chapel marking the place where an ancient icon of Our Lady was discovered, thanks to the vision of an octogenarian nun, Sister Pelagia, in 1822.

The lady to whom he'd been confiding could hardly have been more unlike this memory. He continued to recall, in what must have been just a few seconds, how he'd stopped one of these nuns as she came out of the chapel on the hill, and to Agnes' displeasure, asked her why she was doing penance in that way. He forgot what she began to reply as Agnes had abruptly pulled him away.

The Agnes with whom he was now conversing was human, and totally unlike what he imagined a nun to be. "How come that you are dressed like this?" he finally added. "Sitting and talking as a normal human being? I thought nuns always wore veils and had beads around their waists!"

Agnes laughed. "That went out some time ago," she replied. "Although," she added, "there are some who wear a veil. Usually I wear a cross on a chain around my neck, but I'm on holiday here – like you. There are three of us here staying on the island, but the others wanted to walk up to the Crusader castle ruins. I decided it would be too hot a climb at this time of day. Also, I am not so interested in medieval ruins as they are. I thought a leisurely walk and swim would be preferable. I was going to explain to you," she continued, "that I've spent most of my life in religious communities where we look after sick people: mostly in Africa where we care for AIDS' sufferers. We run centres for them, mostly men, and I'm based in one on the outskirts of Kampala in Uganda, but our headquarters, our Motherhouse, is just outside London."

She paused and Philip was looking at her with renewed interest, bewilderment and surprise. "I came back to England – well Ireland, to be exact, because my mother was very ill. She died just three days after I returned. I was able to be at her bedside as she died, and that was a great blessing. After the funeral my Superior suggested that I take a short holiday with two other of our sisters who were working with deprived families in London. A good friend and benefactor offered to pay for all three of us and suggested we come over here."

"That's fantastic," said Philip after a pause. Then he added, "I suppose I should call you Sister Agnes?"

"Oh no," she quickly responded. "Certainly not here on holiday, and even at home, or in Africa I prefer just my Christian name, although most of the Africans like to tag on the "sister"."

"I'm amazed," said Philip, "and impressed." He lapsed into silence, "To love and to be loved," he found himself softly repeating.

"Yes," he said aloud. "Perhaps that's what's been wrong with my life. Perhaps I didn't really show my love for my wife - perhaps I didn't really love her - and did she really love me? After all, what is love? How does one define it? To love and to be loved - yes, that does make sense. You know, I've missed out somewhere."

The sun was beginning to hover over the western hills of the island.

"I feel like walking back to the hotel. I've enjoyed talking with you, Agnes – Sister Agnes. Maybe we could continue another time. Are you going to have your swim?"

"Yes," said Agnes, "Before the sun goes down. It's been good meeting you. Why don't you join the three of us for dinner tonight? You'll see then that three Catholic nuns can really be quite human. We were going to eat at Marcello's on the harbour. It's the best for fresh fish and not too expensive."

"Thanks, I'd appreciate that. What time?"

"About 7.30pm, English time. Greek time could mean anytime between then and 10 o'clock."

Philip gathered up his belongings and turned to go up the path back to the village, discreetly not turning around to see Agnes preparing to enter the water.

There was a lightness in Philip's step as he walked back. He was thinking over what Agnes had said to him. His wife, Agnes, was as he had described her, but what of himself? Certainly not without faults, not without blame.

Where had he gone wrong in the marriage? Did he really love Agnes? Had he ever really loved her? These were difficult questions to answer.

Then there were the thoughts generated by his encounter with this other Agnes. He'd never been able to open up to anyone as he had to this nun. It was strange, and he had had no idea that she was a nun: a Roman Catholic nun, too. He'd always been a little suspicious of Catholics. It was probably inbred in him coming as a hand-down from Reformation times. It would be interesting, and maybe enlightening, to meet the other two.

Promptly at 7.30pm that evening, he arrived at Marcello's. He was glad it wasn't the taverna he'd previously sampled. He looked around. It was early on the Greek timetable. Most restaurants didn't start functioning in earnest for another hour or so. There were two tables already taken, almost certainly by English holiday-makers, but no sign of Agnes and her friends.

Philip decided to sit down. He chose a table for four nearly at the water's edge. Several small fishing boats were tied to rings in the concrete a few inches from where he had seated himself.

Five minutes went by and he espied Agnes and her friends coming towards him. Agnes was dressed in a bright red blouse with black tight trousers, her short hair set off by a casually draped loose silk multi-coloured scarf around her neck. The others were clad slightly more soberly, but there was little to suggest their calling.

Philip was introduced to Joan and Rita. He wondered what, if anything, Agnes had told them about himself. They had hardly sat down when the waiter gave them each a menu, described in understandable English something about each item, and then invited them all into the kitchen to examine at first hand what the various foods looked like. They each made their choice, resumed their seats and began talking. Subjects touched on a wide range of topics – travel, Greek history, children and young people, the difficulties of teaching, and only occasionally was anything remotely religious mentioned – God and faith and church. People at the surrounding tables – the restaurant had soon filled up – several times turned to look at the three women and the man who frequently were heard laughing quite loudly.

So it was that the leisurely spread out Greek meal passed all too quickly. Philip realised that his problems and questions had not been resolved, but they had assumed a less prominent place in his thoughts. He had enjoyed his evening, perhaps more than any he had spent for some years, and he could hardly believe it had been with three Catholic nuns.

By 11 p.m. all agreed that it was time to retire for the night. They settled the bill. Rita held the purse and refused to accept Philip's offer of help, so he paid for his own separately. "Just wait a moment," Agnes stopped them as they were about to get up.

"I've something I'd like to give you, Philip, as a kind of memento of a most enjoyable evening." She produced from a bag she had concealed under her chair a strange goblet made of pottery. "It's a Pythagorean cup", she explained, although this meant nothing to Philip.

It was similar to a wine glass in shape, fashioned in a rusty brown smooth pottery finish. What was unusual about it was that in the middle of the bowl of the cup was a stem with a small hole which penetrated inside to the base of the cup. Agnes explained that if the cup were filled to the top with water all the water would run out through the hole. However, if it were only partly filled up to a certain point, none of the water would run out, as the air pressure would prevent it. The moral, she went on to explain, was that if you are too full of yourself, too preoccupied with your own concerns, your own needs and desires, then you end up empty.

"An island-hopping young man I met yesterday here at the harbour," continued Agnes, "gave it to me just before he boarded the ferry. He said he'd bought it on Samos where Pythagoras used to live. However, he had decided that he was already carrying too much luggage and he felt he'd learned the lesson of the cup, anyway."

Philip thanked her, they exchanged addresses, and finally parted. It was quite a sad moment, and when Philip had returned to his hotel room, he fell to looking at the Pythagorean cup and thinking of what Agnes had said about it.

Finally, when he had returned home, it would become a visual reminder of his all too brief encounter with Agnes, Joan and Rita, and especially of certain things that Agnes had said to him. His wife, Agnes, had left their home quite suddenly during his absence on Halki. She had taken the two girls with her and left a short note explaining that her departure was definite and she was going ahead with a divorce.

"To love and to be loved," this, and other thoughts, that Philip carried over from his all too brief meeting with Sister Agnes, helped him to realise that the moral of the

Pythagorean cup had to be the key to the future of his life alone, or - was he too full of himself? Perhaps he was........

He was on his own. His work meant that he only occasionally spoke with others. Some of the time he worked from home and there was no one else living in the house. His two children, rapidly becoming independent, only came to see him once a month. The one bright light seemed to be when he exchanged an e-mail with Sister Agnes, who had returned to Uganda. She often encouraged him to follow the lesson of the Pythagorean cup, and it was this that finally, after over a year, caused him to decide to leave his website work, hand over to his deputy director, find tenants for the house, and arrange to fly out to Kampala to help the sisters in their work with the rapidly increasing number of AIDS patients.

He had no skills, but he had at least a willingness to help with some of the very basic needs of those who were dying of this terrible plague. Agnes had warned him of some of the unpleasant things he would have to do, like clearing up the mess each morning as so many, in the last stages of the illness, suffered from severe diarrhoea. The nauseating stench and the unpleasant mess to be cleaned up were a far cry from sitting in front of a clean computer screen.

He found young people there who were dying, and they were asking questions:

"Is there a God?"; "Does he really love me?"; "Why am I here?"; "Why do I have to suffer?"

"To love and to be loved"

Philip was slowly learning to love, not to be full of himself; and he was loved by the poor people he was helping.

He stayed there for nearly eighteen months: eighteen months spent with the poorest of the poor; eighteen months caring for the very basic needs of children, of parents dying of AIDS and leaving their children, who were also infected with the disease.

He couldn't help thinking that this was so different from pictures and commentaries he had seen on the television screen at home where it was often the poor facing the indifferent or unhelpful smile of the rich.

The time slid by and he knew that one day he would have to return home – but he asked himself, where was home? He was with Sister Agnes quite frequently although she was working with a different group of sufferers, mainly women. Their friendship developed and Philip was filled with admiration when he saw how devoted she was to the people she served. There were occasions when they were able to have time together discussing problems and difficulties connected with their work, as well as relaxing together with the other sisters, listening to music or playing scrabble. Their relationship was good and pure and never went beyond the occasional goodnight hug. Agnes clearly enjoyed male company, as did most of the others in the community.

Then one evening, their work finished, several of them were enjoying a mug of tea and sharing anecdotes from the events of the day, when Agnes noticed that Philip was looking particularly pale. She asked him if he felt all right.

"Just a slight headache," he replied. "It's nothing." However less than a minute later he had excused himself and was vomiting in the toilet.

"I think I'll retire to my room," he called out. Agnes, after a few moments, followed him there and insisted on taking his temperature.

"You have a fever," she pronounced, " and I think you may have a touch of malaria. I'll send for the doctor."

The local doctor appeared less than an hour later and confirmed Agnes' diagnosis. Philip became quite ill and was confined to bed for many days, but thanks to good nursing by the sisters, he slowly recovered. Agnes suggested that he returned to England to complete his convalescence.

It was a heart-rending experience leaving the many sick and poor people he had been helping and knowing that, if he did on a future occasion return, most would no longer by there, as death was a frequent visitor. Most of all, however, he was saddened by having to bid farewell to the community of sisters and especially to Sister Agnes.

She had arranged for him to stay for a period of convalescence with the community to which she was attached and which had its centre just outside London. After that he could resume his work, but she felt that a short time spent at this place called Eziat would in every way be of help to him.

She had told him very little about Eziat and so it was with a little apprehension that on arrival in London, he found himself heading immediately on the Central Line to Epping. He was travelling light, but still had in his luggage the Pythagorean cup.

Chapter 7 – Colour

R on Redbridge awoke late one morning in November, sleepily moved across his room to the electric kettle on the table, switched it on and at the same time turned on his computer, which he had only recently saved up for and purchased second-hand.

He was a tall man in his early twenties with broad shoulders and strong hands that indicated that he was no stranger to hard manual work. This indeed was the case as he had just six months previously given up his job as a grave-digger in the public cemetery on the edge of Kingston, Jamaica. This was where he and all his forebears for at least two generations had lived and worked. Grave digging was not very remunerative, and although coffins were not placed low in the ground, it was usually dry and hard.

Often people living in the shanty town bordering on the cemetery would come the night after a burial, unearth the coffin, remove the body, re-bury it and then re-sell the coffin. This was an accepted practice and part of Ron's job had been to ensure that the corpse was properly covered again the following day.

Ron was intelligent and he wanted to improve his lot. He had finally managed to save enough money to pay for his air fare to London. It had meant three years of sometimes going without food for days but he had eventually made it. Arrived in London and following the advice of a fellow Jamaican he had met on the plane, he had found work in a supermarket unloading and stacking boxes and cleaning floors. It was in Shepherds Bush where he had also found a small bed-sitter nearby. On his third day there he had noticed one of the girls at the cash point and had been immediately attracted by her. She was white and he was black.

In Jamaica all his friends had been black and he had never imagined having anything at all to do with anyone other than of his own class and background. However, there was something quite unusual about this particular girl. She was invariably smiling and, as far as he could see when he looked in her direction, she was friendly, chatting to the customers and helping them in a way that he did not observe with others at the check out points. He heard someone calling her Wendy.

One day, when the shop was less busy he managed to be near her and opened up conversation – just a few remarks about their work in the supermarket. Her eyes, he noticed, seemed to light up when he spoke to her and she was more attractive than ever. She had dark hair and deep brown eyes and he noticed her slim figure and beautiful breasts.

She, for her part, had felt sorry for him having to heave boxes from one end of the store to the other, although his manly physique seemed quite equal to it. When he had spoken she noticed that he had a vibrant and melodious voice and spoke English with only a slight trace of a West Indian accent. She was not in the least put off by the fact that he was black.

Ron found that on two days in the week they both finished work at the same time and on one of these occasions they almost collided with each other as they set off for the underground station. They immediately started talking, each feeling easy in the other's presence as they walked together.

Thus was set the beginning of their friendship which rapidly developed into a deeper relationship. They sometimes went off after work and spent hours in a nearby café. Ron found that Wendy was working temporarily at the supermarket during Easter vacation from university in Hull where she was reading social science. This put her in a very different class from Ron who nevertheless was intelligent and had begun to read a lot in his spare time.

Wendy found that she was not only attracted to Ron as a well-built and strong man, but he was kindly and seemed really interested in how she felt and on one occasion when she had a slight migraine he was most attentive. The fact that he was black in no way worried her and she was fascinated by his stories of life in Kingston.

As their friendship grew, Wendy felt it was necessary to tell Ron that she had a friend at university, Ralph, who worked in the library there. Ralph was doing most of the running whereas she herself often became bored with his company. With Ron she felt exhilarated and buoyed up.

On one occasion she took Ron back to the house she shared with three other girls and introduced him to them. She found their reactions interesting, although in one case frightening. One of the girls had said after Ron had gone, "Wendy, I hope you won't be bringing him here again. I really don't think it's good to mix like that with blacks – and besides, he smells."

Then the same girl had added, "you know it wasn't all that long ago that there were notices outside some of the digs in this part of London which said, "No Blacks. No Irish."

The time came for Wendy to return to university where she would be living at home with her mother who was widowed, her father having died of a sudden and massive heart attack when Wendy was still a baby. On their last evening together before Wendy took the train to Hull, she and Ron had talked very seriously about their relationship which, they both agreed, had a deep and lasting quality about it. True, they had only known each other for just five weeks but they had begun to think that it could be for always. So it was on this note that they parted whilst having promised each other that they would be in touch almost daily be e-mail or phone.

Soon after Wendy's return to Hull, she had mentioned her friendship with Ron to her mother who had immediately ranted on about coloured people creating problems with regard to housing, over-occupied hospitals and unemployment, but most of all, when she discerned that Wendy was involved in a serious relationship, she objected to the possibility of having to put up with grand-children who might be black, or dusky-skinned, as she termed it. This diatribe against black people had, if anything, tended to produce the contrary effect hoped for by Wendy's mother.

Wendy's other problem was in relation to Ralph. She decided she had to be open with him and explain the situation. She felt he probably guessed that something was amiss as she had not corresponded or phoned regularly for some weeks. On her second day back she arranged to meet him when he finished work at the library. They walked along the road as far as the bus stop where she would catch the bus home and she, as gently as she could, tried to tell him although she did not mention Ron. He had at first answered nothing and then, with a deep sigh, had said, "Wendy, I've not changed in my feelings towards you. I love you now and will do always. I had just hoped that we might soon move in together. In fact, I can't think of going on living without you. " He continued in this vein for some minutes and then tried to kiss her, but she pulled away.

"Look, Wendy," Ralph continued, "I hadn't told you before, but, as a surprise, I've booked two tickets for the theatre tonight, for you and for me. Please come – and we can then talk more. It's "The Way of the World"." How could she refuse? And he knew that she particularly liked Restoration drama and he was very persistent. Perhaps, after all, she owed it to him to go just this once.

"All right," she said, and as her bus arrived, she hopped quickly onto it and called out, "Call for me at Mum's."

She had intended telling him about Ron, but she had just felt at that moment that she couldn't. She had hurt him enough. It was strange, she thought, that he didn't seem to have guessed that there was someone else on the scene.

She felt she would have to go with him to the theatre. She had been forced into it. She wondered if he really had already bought the tickets. Perhaps tonight she would have the courage to tell him about Ron.

When she arrived home she e-mailed to Ron. She knew it would be useless trying to phone him as he was working late that day. It was the following morning that Ron had got up late, poured out his coffee and sat down in front of the computer. It took some minutes to warm up, and then, as sometimes happened, something went wrong and he was unable to get through to his e-mails. This was not an uncommon occurrence, but it was one that invariably angered Ron. He banged on the table and spat at the screen. Wendy had asked him why he kept a piece of rag by the side of the computer and couldn't believe him when he had told her it was to wipe off the spit from the screen. This he now proceeded to do and after a few more moments he was able to view the letter that had come through.

"My dearest Ron," it began. "I do wish I could see you and talk, although I'll phone tomorrow. I spoke to Ralph this evening. I told him I had changed but I didn't tell him about you. I couldn't honestly, Ron. He says he's lost faith in me and in life generally and he doesn't know what he's going to do. I feel I've hurt him dreadfully and I'm bothered and I'm so tired and afraid for him; and I do wish we were together again."

She had broken off at this point and continued the following morning, an hour or so before Ron was reading it. She continued, "Ralph wanted to take me out this evening, and really I didn't know what to do. He was so insistent, and he seemed so upset, so I agreed. The play was great – "The Way of the World", but it was unfortunate, because of its typical Restoration theme of concealment and in parts where it touched on our own situation. I really don't know whether Ralph was sensitive to this or not. In the end we didn't really talk very much but I think he suspects that there is someone else in the picture, although I still haven't mentioned you, and he wants to see me again, today or tomorrow. Dearest Ron, I'll phone you tonight. My love always, Wendy. XXXXXX"

Ron made himself another mug of coffee. He had an aching feeling inside him. He couldn't bear thinking of

Wendy going out again with Ralph. He thought again of some of the things they had discussed together: the disparity of culture, colour and creed. They had felt that these differences between them could, and indeed, had, already, been overcome. The thought went through his mind, as it had done before, that this Ralph was white, and of a similar educational background. What if Wendy went back to him? It was quite clear that Ralph was still very drawn to Wendy. Yes, he had to admit that her e-mail had aroused a strong streak of jealousy in him. He felt more than ever that he wanted to settle down with Wendy and enjoy a normal married life together. However, that just wasn't possible until Wendy had passed her final exams and he had, hopefully, found more remunerative work.

These, and many other thoughts occupied Ron as he sipped his coffee on that morning. He was impatient. He felt that they really loved each other sufficiently "to make a go of it." Yes, he had to see her again soon and talk it through.

The opportunity to do so eventually came later in June when Wendy had to go to London for an interview. If she passed her final exams she was hoping for a job in the Commonwealth Office. She had been called for an interview and had phoned Ron to tell him that she would travel down very early in the morning. They had agreed to meet at his bed-sitter in Holland Park and go together to the Foreign and Commonwealth Office, in Whitehall.

It was the Monday morning rush hour. Ron and Wendy were standing happily pushed close together. Ron had his arm around Wendy's waist and they were breathing in each other's breath, enjoying their enforced proximity.

Suddenly, the train slowed to a rapid halt just before Queensway station. After a few moments the announcement came over the speaker system that someone had fallen onto the line. Those standing near to Wendy and Ron began to utter comments about the event, until after some fifteen minutes of obvious agitation on the part of some of the passengers who clearly also had appointments to keep, the train finally started moving in reverse.

Fortunately, this did not cause Wendy to be late for her interview which turned out to be not as daunting as she had anticipated. Afterwards they went for lunch and were able to talk about the future.

Ron had already made enquiries about getting a better job as a bus driver. He had learned to drive just before leaving Jamaica and it just remained for him to sort out his PCV licence. There was both a practical and a theory test for this and then, assuming that Wendy was accepted for the Commonwealth Office, they would be able to settle into a permanent and stable relationship.

They talked about marriage. They talked about living together and getting married later. This raised a problem for Wendy who was a Catholic. She had already spoken to a priest about it and he had advised her against it. They also talked about Ralph. "More than half the marriages of couples who have lived together before marriage eventually end in divorce," the priest had told her. When she mentioned this to Ron he had answered with an air of superior knowledge and an "I told you so" look on his face, "That's the sort of attitude I'd expect from a celibate priest. He doesn't know what it is to fall in love with an attractive girl like you...........What right has he to say that we shouldn't share a bed?"

"He's only reminding us of the teachings of Jesus who said "No" to fornication – and that's what it is if we're not married," responded Wendy.

"Yes, but we are committed to each other," replied Ron, "aren't we?" he added. "And that's almost as good as being married, isn't it?"

"We haven't yet made that solemn and final promise," said Wendy.

"No, but soon we will; so what about fixing a date now and that will conclude this discussion. We've talked enough about it, but never come quite to this point. We won't say "soon come" as they do back home and that may mean anytime in the future, sooner or later."

"There's my mother," said Wendy, "I'm sure she would never come. And what about your family?"

"Oh, none of them would be able to come: too far."

"Look Ron," said Wendy, "Why don't we have just a very quiet and simple wedding? No fuss, no guests – well, hardly any. No great ceremony and no great expense. What about it?"

"A great idea," replied Ron somewhat to Wendy's surprise. "I had been thinking on somewhat similar lines," he added, "but I thought you'd be keen on the white dress and all the extras. All we really need are two witnesses."

"Yes, and no flowers or organ or top hats or confetti." Ron was warming to the subject.

"You'd be happy, then," said Wendy, "to have it in the Catholic church? I noticed you mentioned "no organ"."

"Yes, provided your priest wouldn't mind it like that."

"I'm sure he wouldn't," said Wendy. "The priest I've heard of is a very straightforward and simple man. I'm sure he'd agree."

"O.K., then, when should it be?"

"As soon as I've finished at Hull with exams. What about the beginning of October?"

"That's another three months."

"Yes, and it's realistic. It gives you time to get really started on the bus driving and I will be just about to start at the Commonwealth Office."

"It will still seem a long time." Ron paused and then added, slowly, "As long as you promise not to see that Ralph again. You see, I can get quite jealous."

"O.K., that's a deal," she replied, "although," she added, "I feel as though I've done something terrible to Ralph. You know on that early train from Hull this morning I thought I saw Ralph seated at the other end of the same coach. I didn't want to look too closely as the person had his back to me, and then I felt it must have been imagination, or probably someone just like him."

"I wish you could get him out of your mind, you know. Say, let's go and see that priest of yours soon and fix a definite date."

"Right," replied Wendy, "next time I come down to London."

"No," said Ron, suddenly, "let's see him tomorrow before you go back to Hull."

"Well, you know he's a busy man and he may not be available," said Wendy.

"Well, we could go on the off-chance, or phone. Where does he hide out?"

"We might get him at Theydon Bois, near the end of the Central Line or he may, of course, be with his community at a place called Eziat, but that's further on."

"Come on, let's get back to my bed-sitter and phone him."

They returned to Ron's quarters, phoned the priest, making an appointment for the following day. They then discussed at length the possible arrangements for their simple, almost austere style, wedding. Various small decisions were made and then Ron said, "You know, I do understand you, Wendy, even after last night. And I love you. I don't understand God – no one does, but I love you and I don't know enough about Roman Catholicism to consider it any more right than any other way to God. However, there are certain things which my conscience tells me are not in the spirit of Christ and which the RC church endorses. Now, you'll probably think this heretical, but all Christ's life points to the fact that he had not time for sects and denominations. I believe he looks at the world and his Church as not being ruled by standards of different denominations – Protestant or RC or Orthodox, but as souls either believing or still in need of salvation." He paused. "These are views I hold now," he continued, "I know you would never change, and if you consider yourself worshipping God in the only right way, then that's O.K. for you, and I would never ask you to change. I know and you know it would have to be me, and at the moment I don't feel prepared to do so although I think I want to know more about the Catholic Church."

"In that case," Wendy enthusiastically exclaimed, "You could go to see Father Chris. We could speak to him about it when we see him about the wedding."

But Ron quickly rejoined: "No, Wendy, I'm really not ready to talk with a priest. I just want to think things out for myself first. I want to read more of the Bible and really take it in, and then what it says about Christ's Church. Don't forget," he added, "that in wanting me to become a Catholic you're asking me almost to give up some of my basic beliefs, it's like cutting off my right hand – I'd be alive but I'd not be much use without the hand."

"If we had any children," he went on, "then most certainly after we're married, I would definitely consider becoming a Catholic and taking instruction, because there would be other lives besides mine to think of."

"But if after, why not before?" asked Wendy.

"Well, I think I've answered that already as best as I can. I just feel I'm best as I am at present. I feel that I know Christ best as I worship now, and that I serve him best as I am now, but children won't know religious stability or faith at all unless their parents can provide them with it under God in a united front."

"Yes, I see that," replied Wendy, "and I'm sure it will all work out, eventually."

That night they were together for the first time under the one roof. Ron sleeping on the floor and Wendy in his bed. At the time arranged the following morning, they arrived at the priest's house at Theydon Bois. He opened the door, smiled, and immediately invited them in. At that moment his phone rang. "Sit down," he said "I'll leave you just for a moment whilst I answer the phone in the office."

As Ron and Wendy seated themselves, Wendy noticed a headline on the morning paper which lay open on a nearby coffee table. She read "Suicide on the underground," and in smaller print, "A young man threw himself in front of a Central Line train. He was seen by both railway staff and a police officer to run from the stairs across the platform and then jump onto the electrified track just as a train was approaching. He was later identified as a Mr Ralph Roding, a librarian, from Hull. A note was found in his pocket addressed to his former girlfriend.

Wendy, after having read the headline, had picked up the paper and had read the whole news item. She swallowed hard and the tears came to her eyes. "Ron," she said, and by this time her shoulders were shaking and she began sobbing. Ron put his arm around her.

"That was the train we were on yesterday morning," she said.

At that moment Father Chris walked in. "Hello," he said, "What's happened?"

Ron started to explain "and this Ralph Roding used to be Wendy's boyfriend; and," he hesitated, "and she is mentioned in his suicide note."

"I see," said Father Chris. "That's a great shock for you both, and especially for you, Wendy." "You know," he continued, "there are happenings in our lives that we cannot foresee and cannot understand. And we all fail and have regrets, but we have to remember that God makes good our failings; he brings good out of evil: that's the message of the death and resurrection of Jesus. You're bound to wonder, "if only" I had acted differently or if something else had happened, but we have to learn to live with our mistakes and regrets." He paused for a moment and then said, "Shall we pray for a few minutes?"

Wendy nodded. Father Chris continued to pray aloud commending Ralph to the mercy and forgiveness of God, and then praying for Wendy that she might find inner peace and comfort, that Ron would be able to make her happy and that they would each be a support and help to each other.

After a while, he then suggested that they might talk about their forthcoming marriage. They fixed the date for their ultra simple and straightforward wedding ceremony and he advised them to register for a pre-marriage course. They were able to arrange this on the weekends that Wendy was able to travel down to London.

The weeks passed. Ron became fully-employed as a bus driver and moved into a small flat near his former lodgings. For Wendy, the exams were taken and she did not need to wait for her results before starting to work at the Commonwealth Office.

The wedding was arranged, although there was very little arranging to be done. One of Ron's sisters, Geraldine, had decided to come with her partner, Ken, to live in London. They would be the witnesses, and Wendy's mother, after a great deal of humming and hawing, accompanied by caustic comments about the inadvisability of marrying a black person, had finally said she would be present at the wedding. There were still times when she reminded Wendy of what a nice person Ralph had been. It was only three months since the rail incident when Ralph had been killed and Wendy still found it difficult not to think about it with horror and regrets, although she knew that she could never have been happy with Ralph.

On the day of the wedding in early October the weather, surprisingly for England, was bright, warm and sunny and the little church at Theydon Bois provided a welcome setting for it. Two chairs were placed in front of the altar and three at the side. Two candles on the altar were lit and there was a third slightly larger candle between them on the middle of the altar. Ken and Geraldine were already there as also was Wendy's mother, dressed in a bright purple dress and a matching wide-brimmed straw hat which drooped over her forehead and almost hid her eyes. She was trying to ignore the presence of the other two, when Father Chris walked in and went over immediately to speak with her.

"I'm here, but I don't approve of it, you know," she said in a not very quiet voice before Father Chris could say anything. He smiled and told her that, nevertheless, she was very welcome.

He then spoke to Ken who was clutching two simple black rings. They chose them, Ken explained to Father, to remind them of their commitment to the poor. "That's good," and Father smiled, "but be careful not to drop them down that grid. That's what the best man did at a recent wedding in this church."

At that moment Ron and Wendy walked in. Both wore jeans, white tee-shirts and sandals. They came in hand in hand and both looked radiantly happy. Wendy went over and kissed her mother and Ron would have followed suit but Wendy's mother hesitantly held out her hand which he clasped for a second.

There was no organ, not even a guitar, to welcome the bride and there were no flowers on the altar. At first it seemed cold and bare and almost stark and void of any sense of celebration. Father Chris began, in the way he probably began every wedding, by welcoming them, and he then turned to Wendy and Ron and praised them for dispersing with the non-essentials so that the importance of their exchange of consent, the contract and the sacrament of marriage, could be the better highlighted.

"You are giving love to each other. You are giving God to each other," he said. Ron and Wendy looked at each other and smiled and their love became almost tangible. The others, even Wendy's mother, sensed it and began to appreciate and even approve of the simple style of wedding that the couple had insisted on.

They were thus in due course joined together as man and wife and after the usual formalities of signing the register, they all, including Father Chris and even Wendy's mother, adjourned to a nearby pub for a simple lunch.

Conversation flowed easily and Wendy's mother seemed to thaw by the minute. Ron was making a great effort to be kindly and polite to her and she was gradually responding. and as she said afterwards to Wendy, whilst still wishing that he wasn't black, she had to concede that he was quite intelligent, had a good sense of humour and a pleasant manner. Father Chris was chatting to Ken part of the time and both got onto the subject of the state of the world. Ken, who professed no particular religion in spite of Geraldine's adherence to a Pentecostal church in Jamaica, was stating categorically that he felt people should be forbidden to bring any more children into the world, into "this monstrosity of gasses", he said "All they will encounter," he added, "would be sin, misery, death, parting, the fleetingness of love, treachery of friends, tea, cold porridge, superficiality and other like evils!" Ken was almost waxing poetical.

Father Chris clearly couldn't let this pass without comment. "Much of what you say is true, and most suffering and evil is caused by man's misuse of his free-will," he said. "I don't agree, however, that people should be forbidden to have children. It's rather a challenge to parents to have children and to bring them up so that they use their freedom in a right and moral way." Father was clearly warming to his subject, but at that point Ron decided it would be a good moment to thank them for coming and especially for being so co-operative and understanding. He thanked Father Chris especially as well as Ken, Geraldine and Wendy's mum – "my mother-in-law," he couldn't help adding. He then turned to his sister, "Perhaps, Geraldine, you'll pull the stops out when you get married to Ken, here."

"Perhaps I won't..." Geraldine quickly murmured under her breath. Then she went on to say, so that the others heard her, "I may go to the Pentecostal church, but that doesn't mean that I would want a big loud show of a wedding – does it Ken?" and she turned to her partner who nodded in agreement. "Just nice and quiet with a few friends," he said. "When the time comes," he added, smiling.

"You know," said Geraldine, looking at Ron and Wendy, "I'd love you two to come along one Sunday to where I go in central London."

"O.K.," said Ron, "let us know."

At that point Wendy's mother rose from her chair. "Well," she said, "I must say I'm glad, after all, that you invited me and I'm pleased to have met you Ron. I wasn't really looking forward to seeing you, but I've changed my mind – just a little- and I hope you'll make my Wendy happy. I must catch my train back to Hull now." At that she kissed Wendy on both cheeks, shook Ron's hand and nodded to Ken and Geraldine. As she left Wendy thought she saw a tear run down her mother's cheek.

Ron and Wendy settled down to married life which also involved many hours of work for Wendy in the office and for Ron behind the wheel. This latter sometimes involved shift work. However, one Sunday morning they had both gone to Mass together. Sometimes Ron would accompany Wendy and when they returned home would ply her with all sorts of questions about what he had seen and heard. She was in the throes of trying to answer him when Geraldine and Ken arrived.

"I'm keeping you up to your promise to come with me to church," she announced. "Today, in fact now, if you're both free," she said.

"O.K.," said Ron, looking at Wendy, "Is that O.K. with you, Wendy?" Who after a moment's hesitation , nodded, "Yes."

"Boy," said Ron, "that'll be two churches in one day. I am getting religious."

Geraldine led them to a large hall near Marble Arch. It was nearly midday and people of all ages were directing their steps towards the entrance down a side street.

"I sure hope we're not called on to do anything," said Ron as the four of them went in.

They found themselves in a hall which seemed to be attached to an adjacent church. Chairs filled most of it, all facing towards a platform where a five-man music group were already installed with their instruments. One of them, who was clearly the leader, was standing and leading the singing. Ron again whispered to his sister, "Let's keep to the back."

There were probably nearly a thousand almost filling the hall and the sound from the instruments, the singing and the frequent clapping was deafening. After a half-hour the singing stopped and the Leader started speaking. He warned everyone that they were all sinners but nevertheless God loved them and wanted them to repent and follow in the Lord's way. After every few sentences he was interrupted by enthusiastic cries of "Praise the Lord, praise the Lord."

This went on for a further half an hour before the band and the singing started up again. Then the leader in a loud voice announced, "O.K. folks now perhaps we can have a few minutes of silence and just listen to what the Lord has to say to us." A hush gradually spread across the hall and this lasted for no longer than thirty seconds before the voice of a lady sitting near Wendy cried out, "Praise the Lord for this wonderful silence," whereupon immediately the singing and clapping started up again.

At this Ron whispered to his sister, "I think we've been here long enough: I suggest we go." After they had left he said, "I've really had enough of religion for one day. Let's have something to eat." They adjourned to a nearby café where Ron apologised to the others for his previous comments, but it was only Geraldine who might have taken offence. Both Ken and Wendy had also been ready to leave.

For Ron and Wendy, the days seemed to pass very quickly for them both. Their work took up most of their time and often Rob was on shift work which meant that there were some evenings when Wendy was alone in the flat. It was at such times that her thoughts would go back to Ralph and his evident love for her and how he must have somehow found out that she was going to London on that momentous day in order to see Ron. And then the appalling memory of how the train she and Ron were on stopped in the tunnel and she did not know until afterwards that it was on account of Ralph's suicide.........and then the note he had left behind. It was all on account of her. She should have dealt with him more gently and kindly...........or perhaps she shouldn't have encouraged him so much in the earlier stages of their relationship.

These and other similar thoughts left her bothered and upset. She didn't like to unburden herself to Ron. He was so good and kind, and besides he was working so hard in order that they could, as he hoped, save up enough for a mortgage. They would then have a place all their own in which, hopefully, to bring up a family. She didn't wish to burden him with all her imaginings and regrets. But if only.............. Fortunately it was just occasionally that she was weighed down by these thoughts, most of the time she was supremely happy and when they were together in the evening neither wanted to go out. They were just happy in each other's company, chatting and sharing their news. Ron usually had plenty of stories to tell about the passengers on his bus.

He was often on the No 96 route and this went from Acton Green to Piccadilly Circus via Shepherds Bush which was convenient for him. One day, in the rush hour, he recounted to Wendy, there had been, with lots of people standing, a man who had seated himself near the front of the bus who kept up a running commentary in a loud voice for all to hear: "Lovely day, isn't it? Beautiful time of year to see everything in bud," and he went on calling attention to some of the landmarks they were passing. "And you know," went on Ron, "everyone gradually became interested and was smiling. After a while I managed to see him in the mirror. He was short, wore dark glasses and was carrying a white stick. I think," said Ron, "that there must be a moral to that."

In their first months of marriage Wendy and Ron grew rapidly from the stage of falling in love to that of loving. They not only affirmed each other as persons through the wonder and beauty of sexual intercourse – and they were both pleased that they had saved this for after their marriage – but they were able to sustain and affirm each other in many other areas of their shared life together.

Ron, very occasionally, had an outburst of temper, usually when he came home tired and had had a difficult customer on the bus to deal with or, as on one occasion, some youngsters on the top deck kept throwing down the stairs, shoes and items of clothing belonging to one of their number. It was then that, rather than row with Wendy, he would go to the computer, which often didn't work quickly or efficiently, and he would spit at it and swear. This was when the piece of rag kept nearby would come in useful. Invariably he would recover quickly from these short outbursts and be able to sit down calmly for his evening meal with Wendy.

"You know, Wendy darling," he said on one occasion, "we're rare birds in this country."

"What do you mean by that?" she asked.

"Well, I read just now that over half the children born in England are to unmarried mothers."

"At least our children will be part of the minority, won't they dearest?"

"Yes, and when will that be, do you think?"

"I've no idea of course. All I do know, Ron, is that you are quite fantastic when we're in bed. You know, I once heard that Jamaicans were the tops when it came to love-making."

"And you're not so bad yourself," responded Ron.

Their hopes for a child were realised when, just seven months after their marriage, Wendy announced that she was pregnant. This was great news and they were delighted. Three months later when all seemed to be going well they agreed that they should tell Wendy's mother. They had seen her twice since the wedding, once when she had graciously invited them to Hull for a weekend, and on the second occasion she herself had been passing through London and had called in and had a meal with them.

Wendy phoned her mother to tell her the news of the baby. There was a moment's silence at the other end of the phone before her mother replied, "Congratulations! I'd wondered when that would happen. I suppose I'll have to guess what shade of brown – or black – it's going to be."

"Mother!" said Wendy, "I thought you'd got over all that. And anyway he – or she- may possibly be the same colour as Jesus. He was brown," added Wendy.

There was a further pause before she heard. "You know, it's still difficult for me. My friends make all sorts of remarks, too. Anyway, I hope Ron is still making you happy."

"Of course he is. Both of us have never been so happy. It's quite wonderful."

"Good," came the response, "that's what's important."

Autumn approached and the baby, a boy, was born two days before Christmas, with a dusky skin and black curly hair and eyes like his mother's.

Both Wendy and Ron agreed that baby Christopher, as he was to be called, was the best Christmas present they could ever have. He was baptised by Father Christopher early in February. Wendy had given up her job and Ron was earning just enough money for them to survive. Sometimes he would do extra hours at a cleaning job near their flat in order to earn a little more. Time passed quickly for Wendy getting used to looking after a baby, and just as she was thinking of returning to work when young Christopher was a year old and a baby-minder about to come in each day, Wendy became pregnant again, and in due course they had another child, a baby girl, to care for.

It was at this point that one evening, when the children were in bed and for once were quiet, that Ron turned to Wendy and, to her surprise, said, "I think I'd like to go and see Father Christopher. We need to arrange for the baptism of the baby and I'd like to talk to him about possibly becoming a Roman Catholic. "

Wendy, for a moment, was quite surprised at this, as the question had not been mentioned since before their marriage.

"Yes, that's fine," she replied. "I'll make an appointment to see him."

A few days later when they sat in Father Christopher's office, having left the two babies with a neighbour to mind, and having arranged for the date of the baptism, Ron turned to Father and asked him how he could find out more about the church.

"A course of instruction would be good. You could join up with a group later in the year. They would meet each week on a Wednesday evening, and then, at the end of the course, you'd be quite free to choose: to go ahead and be baptised, or not. You see, faith is a gift, a gift that you may or may not be given."

"O.K. Father, I'll subscribe to that. Let me know when I can start."

"Perhaps the first thing for you to do," continued Father Christopher, "is to pray together," and he looked at Wendy. "You see the first church is your home. Wendy," he said, "you could also start going to Mass regularly. Bring the children. There's a crèche if they get noisy, and the priest in the parish here doesn't mind children's noise."

Wendy turned slightly red when he reminded her, as a Catholic, of the obligation of going to Mass each Sunday.

"Anyway," concluded Father Christopher, "see what you can do."

Months passed, the baby was baptised, Ron followed the course of instruction; he and Wendy occasionally sat together in the evening, hand in hand in silence, each aware of God's presence with them, and sometimes sharing their prayer. However, when it came for Ron to make a decision about becoming a Catholic, he hesitated. "I've problems," he would say. "There are some things I'm not sure of," he confided to Wendy. "One is this whole question of birth control. We practise contraception now and Father says we shouldn't, but you don't seem to worry about it. We've already talked about this, and you've always left it to me. Then," he went on, "there's a woman in the group at the church who clearly thinks I shouldn't be there. She doesn't approve of any foreigners coming to live in England – neither "Eastern Europeans, Muslims or black people," she said on one occasion. Now I don't think that's very Christian. And she's soon going to be baptised a Catholic."

"Perhaps you should speak with Father Christopher about these things," Wendy replied.

"And then," he continued, "there are so many problems in the world where religion seems to be the cause of divisions and violence. Look at the crusades, and today the problems there've been in Ireland, in Iraq and dozens of other places."

"Yes, but I don't think you can say that religion is the cause of some of these terrible happenings." Wendy suddenly then had an inspiration and she added, "Otherwise it's rather like blaming hooliganism on football. There would be hooliganism without football if there were no football."

"Well," said Ron, "I think I'll just leave it for the time being. "Follow your conscience," is what Father Christopher also said."

That was the end of the conversation. With occasional traumas and the usual ups and downs of married life, three years passed since they had first gone to see Father Chris, and one day Wendy and Ron received a letter from him inviting them to visit him and his community at Eziat. This, he explained, was only a short distance beyond

Theydon Bois where they had got married and where the two children had been baptised. They had to take the Central Line train to Epping and then walk. He also explained that he was no longer helping in the church at Theydon Bois but spending all his time at Eziat with his community.

So it was that one day in June, Wendy and Ron, with the two children, for Father Chris had told them to bring them along too, were on the train to Eziat. They had no idea what they would find there, nor the experience they would have.

Chapter 8 – Eziat

The Central Line train was due to arrive at its destination, Epping, at 11.30am. It was the twentieth of June. Earlier in its journey through central London it had been full, but now most people had got out and there were empty seats in all the coaches. In one of the front coaches there were just seven people and two small children. All, except the two children, seemed to be either buried in thought or looking at one or another of their fellow passengers.

Two men, who were occupied in this way, were seated diagonally opposite each other and, for a moment, they caught each other's eye. A slight smile flickered across the face of the older of the two. "I think I've seen you somewhere before," he said.

"Yes," said the other, a young man. "Was it on this same train some years ago when it was held up in the tunnel?"

"And you were going to Corsica – I remember the label on your luggage," added the older man.

"Yes – you've an incredible memory," said the other.

"By the way, my name's Philip, I'm not wearing my name tag today: off duty."

"And I'm Damian. I'm also off work; just back from the Philippines and I'm going to a place called Eziat."

"That's very strange: I'm going there too," Philip replied.

At this point a smartly-dressed lady looked across at them: "Did I hear you say you were going to Eziat?" she asked in a loud voice.

"Yes, do you know it?" said Philip.

"No, but I'm going there as well," she replied.

An elderly lady, who seemed to be accompanied by a young man, turned around from where they were seated and the lady said, "How very extraordinary, we're going there also. It's a religious community, isn't it?"

"It sure must be," a deep voice came from further down the coach. It was a tall black man who seemed to be with his wife and two children.

At this, as the train stopped for a moment at Theydon Bois, they all by unspoken accord, moved up together and started talking. They compared notes and all agreed that they had been on the same train three years previously on the 20th June when it had been delayed because of an accident at Queensway.

"By the way, I'm Gordon," remarked a quietly-spoken young man who was with the elderly lady who had said she was Betty, "I'm sure, we were, all of us, in that very same coach on that day."

"Yes I remember several of you," said Clothilde who had also introduced herself. "And here we all are," she continued, "all going to the same place that none of us knows. It really is remarkable – an extraordinary coincidence."

"Yes," added the black man who proceeded to introduce himself as Ron and his wife, Wendy, with the two children, Christopher and baby Grace. "My guess is that we're probably all going to see Father Chris. Is that so?" They all nodded, looking even more puzzled. Then he added, "He's a great priest: he married us and baptised these two."

"I will actually be staying there for a while as I'm convalescing from an attack of malaria," said Philip.

At that point the train arrived at Epping and they all got out. The map of the locality displayed at the entrance to the station showed a large green area with several black rectangles on it, the whole being marked "Eziat". It was just a short walk eastward from the station.

They set off and continued their discussion about their unusual encounter. Was it just a strange coincidence or was it, as Damian had suggested, and some of them seemed to agree, Divine Providence? As they walked along, passing rows of suburban homes, the path soon ascended to a plateau on the edge of which was a small brick building and by the door a large notice which spelt out "Welcome" in seven different languages.

Several young people were seated at a table next to the notice and smilingly greeted the newcomers who were each presented with a small spray of wild flowers. They were told that they could see Father Christopher after the midday prayer. At that moment a loud peel of bells from a nearby archway put an end to conversation, and they were instructed to go towards the church which they now noticed was situated beyond the archway with the bells.

All sorts of people of different nationalities, colour and cultures were already coming from all directions and entering the church, which from the outside looked more like a bleak factory building. However once inside, and their eyes having become accustomed to the dim lighting, it took on a different appearance. Down the centre there were two long rows of chairs and prayer stools. These were slowly being occupied, one by one, with white-habited men on one side and women in pale blue, on the other. Soft classical music was being played, interspersed with live organ music played by another white-habited individual seated in a small gallery high up in the wall. Small candles were burning at one end of the building illuminating a large wooden cross on which was painted an icon of the crucified, risen and glorified Christ.

The church was rapidly filling up and within minutes several thousand people had gathered, most of them young and seated cross-legged on the coarse-carpeted floor or on prayer stools, whilst the older people, or those who were disabled, sat on benches around the sides. The group who had met on the train managed to find a bench against the wall.

The bells had stopped ringing, a clock sounded midday and all began singing a short repetitive chant. Most seemed to be quite familiar with the words and melody, whilst others followed it from a book where it was printed in several different languages. This went on for some minutes and then one of the white-clad figures arose from his kneeling position and went to a lectern where he read a short passage from the bible. The group from the train, with the exception of Betty, all immediately recognised the reader: it was Father Chris.

He read from St Paul's letter to the Christians in Philippi; "I have learnt this secret, so that anywhere, at any time, I am content, whether I am full or hungry, whether I have too much or too little. I have the strength to face all conditions by the power that Christ gives me."

This was then read in six other languages by others of the white-clad figures. The silence which followed the reading was solid: not a murmur or whisper or sound of any sort pervaded the vast church. All were deep in profound meditation and prayer which was only broken after some ten minutes or so by an instrumentalist introducing the next chant.

To the utter amazement of Gordon he heard the words "The Lord is compassion and love" being repeatedly chanted to a slow and haunting melody.

All joined in except Gordon who was completely stunned by the words of the chant which had set off in his mind the whole series of events that seemed to have dovetailed into his life.

An atmosphere of peace and calm spread through the whole gathering. More singing followed, together with prayers in various languages until the whole white-clad community rose and moved towards the exit. Everyone else then also moved slowly and without haste towards the various doorways. Betty, Gordon, Philip, Damian, Clothilde, Ron and Wendy and the two children, who had been amazingly quiet, all followed suit. Gordon was still astonished by the singing of the refrain, "The Lord is compassion and love," but the expression of surprise turned to awe as he got up and looked up at the roof of the church. It was a vast series of pyramidal shapes which immediately took him back to the cave in Cappadocia and the conversations he and Andrew had had whilst there, together with his own strange experience. He was dazed by it all, but by this time they had all come out into the daylight and there was Father Christopher, having disrobed, and now clad in light trousers and an open-necked shirt, waiting for them.

"I spotted you all in the church," he said, "and I guessed you'd come out by this door."

He greeted them individually as they introduced themselves. "Yes, Clothilde," he said, "I think I heard of your husband from a friend of mine. I'm pleased to welcome you here. And yes, Damian, you and I already know each other. It's good to see you again. Ah Philip, yes Sister Agnes told me, of course, that you were coming. I do hope staying here for a while will help your recovery. Malaria is a horrid illness. Wendy and Ron: how are you both and these two cherubs? They were so good during the prayer." At that point the two children woke up and Grace began to cry. Father Chris moved on to Gordon and Betty, who explained to him briefly the events leading up to the discovery that they were related through Betty's sister-in-law in Australia and how he had come to meet his real mother. Then there was the even more extraordinary way in which he and Andrew had met up with the bard-tramp Francis Buckhurst-Hill, and then in Turkey had been given his notebook with the mention of Eziat.

"Yes, that certainly is quite amazing," replied Father Chris. "I remember Francis, the Irish bard. He was a great character and called here quite a few times over the years. You know," he went on to say, "the way these events have happened in your lives, Betty and Gordon, and, indeed in all your lives in different ways, is a sure sign of God's guiding hand. There can be no other way of accounting for them." He paused for a moment, but before anyone could comment he said, "The Hungarians have a beautiful expression for welcome: 'Isten Hozott' which means 'God brought you here.' Anyway, before we talk further, I suggest that we eat – you can join the community for our midday meal, that is if you don't mind sharing it with us. We eat in silence, and then afterwards we can catch up on all our news and have a really good talk." They were all very happy to go along with this and accompanied him to the community refectory. Everyone else was moving towards various queues that had formed for a self-service meal served from different stone or concrete buildings at different points over the whole area, some half-hidden amongst the surrounding trees and bushes.

The lunch was simple – lentils, carrots, a slice of ham, bread and an orange. All members of the community ate together, although the men and women were at separate tables. Father Christopher introduced his guests to a man who seemed to be the superior. He was white-haired and was the only one who had continued wearing his habit after coming out of the church. He had deep blue twinkling eyes and exuded an ambiance of calm and peace. He warmly welcomed them and, before they were seated, all prayed together:-

"For food in the world where many walk in hunger;

For faith in the world where many walk in fear;

For friends in the world where many walk alone,

We give you humble thanks, O Lord."

The meal was in silence, after which Father Chris led his guests to a small room near the archway with the bells. He half perched himself on the corner of a small table that seemed at any moment poised to topple over. As the others sat down, they were anxious to ask Chris some of the questions that were bubbling up in their minds.

Clothilde was the first to speak: "It really is most extraordinary," she said. "We were all on the same train three years ago not knowing one another, all nervous and worried because it had stopped in the tunnel ....and here we are all together again..........I don't understand it..........And now," she added, "We've just been on the same train again and this time we've all been coming to the same place – here.......I don't understand it. It's really most amazing."

They were still reflecting on how some of them had become, as it were, linked together through a chain of events and how they had all arrived at the same time at Eziat. Betty, who had discovered that her sister-in-law, Sarah's, illegitimate child had been adopted by none other than her doctor and his wife. And then there was Alf, whom she had met in Australia and whose daughter Shirley, had known Damian in Corsica of all places. Philip was remembering how he had noticed the Corsica label on Damian's rucksack and this had set him off thinking about a break, not in Corsica but on a Greek island and through this had met Sister Agnes, gone to Uganda, and ended up about to convalesce here at Eziat. Wendy and Ron had known Father Chris through their wedding and his help when they'd heard of Ralph's death. Clothilde thought of her meeting, although it could hardly be termed a meeting – her encounter with Harry on the Paris metro and then how she had vaguely remembered his mention of the priest with whom he had thought he could talk, a Father Christopher, and the dream she had had a few days before.

They all, each in turn, began sharing these experiences with Father Chris and each listened attentively to the others.

As the last one ended Clothilde, once again, was heard to exclaim, "Extraordinary....quite extraordinary! It's positively uncanny!"

"Perhaps we might ponder together for a few minutes on some of the events that you have experienced and ask ourselves what is meant by these so called coincidences." It was Father Chris who broke in on their thoughts. He continued, "Nearly everyone can relate stories of what they would call chance happenings, coincidences, or, to use a slightly more technical word, synchronicity. It is really when two or more events occur which are mysteriously linked together. Jung, the great Swiss psychologist, called it a "meaningful coincidence." That is to say, there's a connection that cannot be explained by direct causality. Are you still with me?" he asked.

"Yes," replied Damian, "and we've all experienced just that."

"There was also the occasion," he added, "when I had to go to Dr Farthing, who is also Betty's doctor and Gordon's adopted father, and have my eczema treated and through that met Mrs Smith who enabled me to go to the Philippines. He paused for a moment and then added, "Is it just chance? Is there an underlying meaning, a pattern?"

"I'm glad you've asked that question," responded Father Chris. "Yes, I think there is a pattern and a guiding force that brings certain events together. This is exactly where God comes in. There's a pattern to our lives –true we often spoil it through our sinfulness and weakness and blindness, and for us it's rather as though we are looking on the underside of a beautifully woven carpet. We cannot appreciate the pattern. One day we will."

"But so often events don't turn out as they were meant to." It was Wendy who spoke, and immediately Ron continued, "That train we were on – the first time three years ago – when it stopped in the tunnel. The man who'd thrown himself onto the line and was killed was Wendy's boyfriend, before she married me. We've already talked with you about that. And we didn't know this until afterwards. It was terrible."

"Terrible," echoed Wendy.

"Yes," said Father Chris, "that certainly was a frightening experience for you both. However you have to remember, as I've mentioned to you on a previous occasion, that God brings good from evil when we turn to him in faith and love."

"Yes, but what about Ralph?" asked Wendy.

"Ralph despaired, gave up, like Judas in the Gospel. If he'd turned to God in his distress, his jealousy and his anger, he might have been able to bring great good out of the situation. It's for you now, both of you, to bring good from that event. Maybe, and I'm only guessing, you could one day help other youngsters – and there are unfortunately so many – who are tempted to take their lives. I heard recently that there are over five thousands suicides in this country each year. And already, I'm sure you are helping to form these two lovely children in the ways of love………..and aren't they being so good whilst we're talking?" The youngest one had fallen asleep whilst the two-year old was fascinated by the candle lit on the table near Father Chris.

"Coincidence, you see," he continued, "should be termed Providence. This means that God is behind everything, not necessarily directly, and certainly not in the form of a super magician, but often indirectly, sometimes through the laws of nature, of creation, through telepathic communication or even through dreams, clairvoyance and some of those gifts which I believe mankind possessed at the dawn of the world. Someone once said, and it may be true, that thought energy never completely vanishes; thought waves will go out into space; they will diminish but never completely vanish in the whole of time. In fact, nothing we ever do or say or think completely disappears, it goes out into space and into time. That's an arcane thought, isn't it?"

At this Gordon, who, like the others had been listening attentively, exclaimed, "That could possibly explain several of the experiences I've had at different times," and he went on to recount the happenings at Dorchester Abbey and Fountains and the way he and Andrew had met Francis Buckhurst-Hill, and how it was really through him and the few words in his notebook, that he Gordon, had come to Eziat.

"Yes, there are many happenings we do not understand and we can only guess at the truth and then we may be wrong. However, in the case of your friend Francis, I think God was clearly guiding you and wanted to bring you here."

"In that case," Damian interrupted, "I think God has very clearly been guiding you, Father, because, after all, you have been a sort of focal point in all this."

"Maybe, maybe," Chris replied. "I would like now," he continued, "to share with you while you're all together, something about Eziat because I know you were all curious as to what you were going to find here. What I am about to say may just help you in understanding better the pattern and how it may be unravelling in all our lives.

Eziat, you see, is a community of people of all ages, of different nationalities and cultures and we try to centre our lives in Christ, whom we believe is God, dwelling amongst us. By coming amongst us two thousand years ago he showed us something of his own nature and that told us something about ourselves."

"I don't quite follow that," interrupted Gordon. "What did he tell us about God? Was it all about numbers and pyramids and triangles – because I think I'm beginning to understand that."

"Not exactly, although that is a part of his creation. No, he showed us that God is a Trinity. Let me put it in this way. I think it's easier if we start with ourselves. We, you and I, function as a trinity. If, for example I am an artist and I'm going to paint a picture, if I'm a good artist, I'll first of all think of what I'm going to paint –that's what you might call "the idea". I then paint it, I put the idea that was in my mind on to the canvas. That's the "action" or "incarnation" the making flesh of the idea. I then look at what I've painted and others see it, and if I'm satisfied with what I've done, you might say I like it or even love it.

This trinity of thought, action and love operates in everything we consciously and deliberately do – and here we have an image of God where these three exist in perfection: Father, Son and Holy Spirit. It follows, then, that whenever we perform even the smallest and most insignificant action well, to the best of our ability, we're reflecting something of God; we are, as it were, caught up in God, in that movement of love which is God. Most of all is this true when we use our creative skills, but it applies to all our actions if done with love and enthusiasm."

"I'd never thought of it that way," said Damian and Clothilde added, "That takes time to sink in. I've never heard belief spoken of like that before."

"Yes," continued Father Chris, who was clearly warming to his subject, "the problems arise because we often don't act with love and we're not caught up in God. That's when sin and imperfection enter in. The action doesn't correspond to the thought. St Paul wrote on one occasion, the good thing I want to do, I never do; the evil thing which I do not want – that is what I do. That applies to us all, but that is really the basis of our faith here at Eziat, and I wanted to say that, before telling you about the more obvious and practical details of our lives in this community.

It can really be resumed in the words that Gordon thought he heard when he was in Dorchester Abbey and in the Phythagorean cup that Philip was given by Sister Agnes. Let me explain.

First of all those words taken from one of the psalms, The Lord is compassion and love tell us something about Jesus and hence about God himself. On one occasion Jesus told us to seek and then we would find and he said this with regard to prayer: prayer in which we open our hearts to God. This is an adventure and a means to it is through meditative prayer with others: repetitive chants where the words sink into the depths of our being; they become a part of us and then we become immersed in the silence that follows. We all ask questions, we are all seekers and it is through prayer, and in particular silence in prayer, being still in the presence of God, that we little by little begin to appreciate the meaning of life and that the carpet does have a pattern which will one day be discernible."

By this time Father Chris was in full swing and enthusing over his subject, "There is the example of the cup attributed to Pythagorus," he continued. "Philip knows all about it, but for the benefit of the rest of you, it's a cup which forces you to drink only in moderation. If you fill it too full, in fact over half full, the entire contents of the cup empty out through a hole at the bottom. It serves as a warning not to be greedy, not only in what one drinks, but in every aspect of our lives. Philip, I'm sure you realised the importance of this when you were working with the poor in Uganda. If there's just a little for ourselves, then there's more for those in need and who perhaps have nothing.

I think that helps us to appreciate what we're here for, on this earth, I mean.

A great Christian writer and scientist, Teilhard de Chardin, once wrote:

God did not will individually (nor could He have constructed as though they were separate bits) the Sun, the Earth, Plants or Man. He willed his Christ, and in order to have His Christ He had to create the spiritual world, and man in particular, upon which Christ might germinate; and to have Man he had to launch the vast process of organic life (which accordingly Is not a superfluity but an essential organ of the world;) and the birth of that organic life called for the entire cosmic turbulence.

That's the most fantastic vision of the meaning of life, of the world and the place of Christ himself." Father Chris looked around at his audience. They still seemed to be listening, except for the two children who were now curled up asleep close to their parents.

"There were several reasons that brought each of you here today, one was probably curiosity but also, maybe deep down, there was the wish to be happy and at peace. The secret of it is in what I've been saying and Jesus spelt it out clearly in the Gospel and especially in the Sermon on the Mount. I once knew someone who cut out those three chapters from Matthew's Gospel and kept them always in his wallet to refer to frequently. He said to me once that the most important instruction in it was when Jesus told us not to speak to anyone about our good deeds or the ways we showed our love and compassion for others.

One great spiritual writer recently expressed something of what I have been saying in this way." Father Chris picked up a book at his side and began reading:-

'How difficult it is to devote ourselves to prayer and meditation! I know some young people in a meditation group who have been trying to spend half an hour each day in silent prayer. If you ask them how easy it is, they will tell you that it is very difficult. Nevertheless, out of experience they recommend others not to turn silence into emptiness, which has to be filled at any price. Put your book aside and turn off the music. Sink into yourself. Only if you do this will the most important things be revealed to you and will you see the source in which you will find your origins. Those who are capable of being present to themselves in this way in prayer will find that in everything they do and say later, they will achieve a power which is almost limitless. Their language can become light and fire, and all their activity will prove effective. Why, because they have immersed themselves in their being there; they have concentrated their thought, breathing, speech, action and being; and this

concentrated power of being releases energy, so that their words and actions become amazing powerful.

A saint is a person who has found the unity of his or her being and who radiates and becomes effective from this focal point. His or her gaze penetrates others and moves them deeply; his or her words can quite simply move mountains, change society, help us to renew our world.'

We are not saints, but nevertheless this is what we try to achieve here at Eziat. The majority of people live in the opposite way, preferring distraction and dispersion which means that they apply only five or ten percent of their true being to what they are doing and saying. That is why their activity is often so superficial and ineffective.

We have found in our community here that the way to peace and joy and happiness is to centre our lives in God through prayer, and then through this to allow God's Spirit to work in, and through us in our activity, our unselfish love of all. Each one of us is on a journey, a journey through the tunnel to the light. Each one of you has taken a step or two towards the light. Keep going. It's an exciting journey, an adventure not without pitfalls and setbacks and unanswered questions. But you must keep going.

There, I think I've spoken long enough and you've been very attentive. In a few moments I'll leave you and then I hope you'll stay for the evening prayer. Remember where the Central Line has led you and come again."

At that Father Chris finished and quietly left them with their thoughts. No one was inclined to speak. After a while the bells once again began to peel. It was time for evening prayer.

As they all came out of the small building where they had been listening to Father Chris a big man over six foot tall emerged from a nearby room, stopped, stretched up his arms, expanded his chest, and announced to the world in a deep, loud voice, "I love the air here, it's good."

Everyone was now going once again into the church. The singing started, followed again by a reading from the Bible,

"So do not worry; do not say, "What are we to eat? What are we to drink? What are we to wear?" It is the gentiles who set their hearts on all these things. Your heavenly Father knows you need them all. Set your hearts on his kingdom first, and on God's saving justice, and all these other things will be given you as well. So do not worry about tomorrow: tomorrow will take care of itself."

And then silence.

The group who had been with Father Chris were still reflecting on all that he had said. Each of them was feeling that their lives were in fact taking on a particular shape. With some it was still very vague and uncertain, but with others there was a greater certainty.

Clothilde, still haunted by the thought of her husband, Harry, had decided that she would give her spare time, and perhaps eventually all her time, to the care of alcoholics. There was a centre she had heard of in London and she would contact them. Through that, she might one day encounter Harry again and there could be healing - they would perhaps be like two people meeting on the middle of Monet's bridge.

Betty was thinking of her time in Australia, of the way she had unexpectedly been of help to Sarah, and the extraordinary link with Gordon, and now she didn't know what she would do. She looked around her in the church: so many people from so many different countries and the community itself seemed to be made up of different nationalities. Perhaps she could offer her help several days a week with the welcoming of visitors, just as she had been welcomed. Yes, she would speak to Father Chris about that. She could also help with the children, although Wendy and Ron's children seemed so quiet and contented and sleepy, but there were others who were being looked after in a crèche outside the church.

Wendy was feeling that there was little they could do differently in response to Father Chris's talk but to her surprise Ron had suggested as they were walking back towards the church, that when at home it might be good to start to pray together and to do it once a day, if possible, at the same time as all these people who were praying at Eziat. She had taken his hand and squeezed it and said softly, "Yes, let's …and," she had added, " we could come here sometimes to pray with the community. The children seemed to like it; they were so quiet."

In the mind of Damian the priesthood had become somewhat blurred. Through his experience in the Philippines, and now his encounter with the community at Eziat, he felt that God was clearly leading him in that direction. He would have to speak about it further with Father Chris.

Philip had been equally moved by all that Father Chris had shared with them but felt that he would have to resume his work in the city. However, he had first to recover completely from the malaria. Then he thought of the message of the Pythagorean cup: selfishness and greed, or service of others, especially those in need. Perhaps eventually, he would offer his help here with some of the administration and the support of their offshoots working with the poor in other countries. Yes, that was the answer for him. Maybe they would accept him as a permanent helper and he could live there.

Gordon was still musing on the many strange events that seemed to have led up to this visit to Eziat. He almost felt that he was dreaming. Were these others around him real? He wished he could have shared it, as he had done before, with Andrew. He wasn't so sure of some of the points Father Chris had mentioned, but in spite of that, he was impressed by the sight of the white and blue-habited community and of what must have been over four thousand, mostly young people, gathered in the church. He thought of the youngsters of mixed backgrounds whom he was teaching in the east end of London. It would be good to bring some of them here to Eziat. It would be a great experience for them. Yes, he'd have to arrange that. And then he'd have to think about that quotation of Father Chris's about creation. It seemed to link up with his own ideas. Perhaps too, there was something in this idea of God guiding certain events – providence. Yes, in spite of all the evil and hatred reported in the news, in spite of it all, love, a binding force was really at work, taking one up into that strange Trinitarian God, of which Father Chris had spoken. He would have a lot to share with Andrew when they next met.

They were singing once again the haunting chant "The Lord is compassion and love." Gordon joined in with the others.

When the prayer was ended, they all by unspoken agreement remained on in the church until everyone had gone. Wendy had picked up a prayer card as she had entered. She looked at it. It was a picture of St Alban the first English martyr and his feast day was given as the 20th June, that very day.

Meanwhile Betty took from her shoulder bag the prayer she had read just before her husband, Edward, had died:

"Father, I abandon myself into your hands;
do with me what you will.
Whatever you may do, I thank you:
I am ready for all, I accept all…"

Also available from the same author

SHADES OF WELCOME (2002)
ISBN 978-184426-007-2

Available from all good booksellers or
www.upfrontpublishing.com

Also available from the same author

STRETCH OUT YOUR HAND (2005)
ISBN 978-184426-254-5

Available from all good booksellers or
www.upfrontpublishing.com